The Stone

By

Aaron Ross

Copyright © 2019 by Aaron Ross

ISBN 978-1-7341783-0-2

First published November, 2019

Cover art copyright © Aaron Ross

Cover Art created by Takbom Heogh

This book is dedicated to my wife, Michele, who is always in my corner, even when I'm wrong. She is my rock, the wind in my sails, and my muse.

Many thanks to Michele, Michael, Adam, Jesse, Myra, Vanessa, Ryan, Brent, Russ, Brian and everyone else who read my rough drafts for all the support and criticism.

Prologue

During their trip through the Choco, Jim, Johnny, and Mustache had asked themselves, what idiot wears a suit to the jungle? It had been a few days by jeep from Bogota through the rainforest on muddy paths that couldn't be called roads. They had gotten stuck more than once. Jim wondered to himself if they had made the right decision going out into no man's land, Colombia.

Eventually, they found themselves in a small, make-shift village that existed only to process coca leaves into the white powder that sold like gold. Jim got along with the other two, and Ramirez, one of the leaders of the village, but he didn't like any of them. When you're a drug dealer or a pimp, how many people can you really like? Jim was both, and worse. So, with few exceptions, he didn't like anyone. He viewed the three men who were his main companions out in the green as little more than opportunities. They were acquaintances who had mutual interests.

Still, they spent time together, both on the trip to nowhere and in the village itself while they negotiated a deal. They drank and played cards. They argued overpricing and timetables. Ramirez made sure his guests had access to plenty of drinks, product, and women. It was less than a week before they came to an agreement. Still, it was too slow. Had it been even a day earlier, things would have turned out different. The three men were standing by a Jeep getting ready to leave. They were discussing their future meeting with the boss when the world exploded.

Jim barely had a chance to react to the sound of shots fired when Johnny went down. The loud staccato bursts had started and there was a spray of red. Crimson blossoms sprang from Johnny's shirt and parts of his head broke open in fans of bone and blood. Jim could see the wide-eyed look of surprise Mustache gave him as they both dropped to their knees while turning to face the sound. Johnny's body twitched a couple of times next to them and then went limp.

Flares of fire and smoke lit up the shadows of the jungle on the far side of the clearing. Gasoline drums used to soak coca leaves sprang leaks as bullets hit them. One drum caught on fire. A grenade or perhaps a gasoline drum exploded catching a thatched building alight. Bloodied and dead people fell into the brown leaves and mud that made up the forest floor.

In seconds, the drug processing center they were in became complete pandemonium. Colombian rebels could be seen at the edge of the village, coming through the foliage, and pouring into the spaces between buildings. Their clothes were dirty and many of the rifles were rusty. The jungle moisture was not kind to guns, but they worked well enough. The drug dealers that lived there fought back. For at least a minute, the thundering sounds of combat were all that anyone could hear. The rattling weapons belched fire and smoke. The smells of gunpowder, blood, and gasoline mixed together in an overpowering stench.

Jim and Mustache had pulled their weapons out and been firing. The truth was, though, the rebels and the dealers they were there to meet looked too alike to tell apart. Shooting anyone who came near them, they looked for cover too late. One of the Colombians opened up in their direction with an AK. Jim felt something like a baseball bat hit his leg knocking him onto his back. Stunned, he laid there in the jungle mud for a second while the feeling in his leg turned to an intense burning. Deafened by the combat, Jim watched Mustache silently flop over dead as he too was hit.

Watching his last partner die was enough to stir him into action. It wasn't concern for his companions but fear for himself that gave him energy. In a burst of adrenaline, Jim pulled himself up through the shock and pain, then launched himself into the jungle behind. A last glance back saw most of the village burning from the ambush. One of the dealers lay dead, maybe Ramirez, bleeding on a pile of cocaine bricks. Bullets chased Jim into greenery striking trees and bushes. Rushing headlong into the rainforest, he disappeared.

Jim ran.

Through the burning, then throbbing pain in his leg, he ran. The gunfire behind him was sporadic and then stopped. Still, he ran. After a while, he slowed and looked down at his leg. Blood ran from thigh to shoe staining his pants. What idiot wears Armani to the jungle? he thought. Shaking his head and taking his shirt off, he tied it around his leg above the wound. The burning had gone and in its place was a heavy, deep, throb of pain. It felt like a bad bruise.

The shock had worn off. Jim limped slowly as the pain threatened to overwhelm him. Knowing nothing of the jungle, only that death was behind, he went forward. One day turned to two, then three. With no food or water, he survived by drinking the rain that gathered in the wide leaves that made up so much of the jungle floor. By the third day, his wound was infected. It was causing a fever and had begun dripping a sickly, white pus.

The morning of the fourth day found Jim lying up against a fallen tree. The rotten stink of his infected leg in his nostrils, his body was almost too weak to move. Knowing he was done for, Jim decided that this was as good a place as any. Then the leaves rustled slightly as a breeze picked up. A sound of whispers could be heard on the wind, men talking, but too faint to make the words out. Yet he could hear them. That he had made it this far was a testament to his will. Three days in the jungle with no food and little water was proof of that. Unable to stand on his wounded leg, he summoned what was left of his mental strength.

He crawled. He dragged himself through the mud and underbrush towards the whispers carried in the air. He could cry out for help, but no one answered when he did. The whispers remained. And so, he pulled himself forward, hour after hour, leaving a trail in the dirt and grime behind him. Almost spent, he pushed through some brush and found himself in a wide clearing. A stepped pyramid was before him and the path up was a mere few feet away.

The whispers were louder now. He could hear them from the top of that structure. There was a faint blue light glowing at the apex. No one answered his calls. Delirious and too weak to stand, Jim was still a man of will.

Calling on the strength he had left, he pulled himself up the first step of the pyramid and began climbing.

Chapter 1

The Man

His name was Jim Jones, and he was the only man I ever knew who didn't squint into the rain. Most people walk around in the cold, arms tight and leaning into the wind, their eyes squinted for protection. Not Jim, though. He walked upright, head high and blue eyes observing the street like he owned the city, the wind, and the wet. And he was dry when he came in out of it.

He wasn't always like that. The first time I noticed anything was different, I was too happy to see him. He came in off the San Francisco streets with a little of The Bay mist following him. His short, black hair and clothes were dry then, but I was too busy giving him a hug and letting the other boys shake his hand to pay attention. No one thought anything of it. We were just glad to have him back. At least most of us were.

Jim had been gone for almost thirteen weeks, and we thought he was dead. He had gone down to Columbia with a couple of Lanza's boys to secure a source of coke to sell. Lanza was the head of the mob in San Francisco, the capo, The Boss. Since we paid Lanza to work in his city, did jobs for him, he had gifted us with the opportunity to help expand his business. Jim was our crew's leader, sometimes thought of as a junior lieutenant to Lanza, and had been offered the chance to head to Bogota. He went with "Mustache" Caruso and Johnny Vaccaro a couple of senior guys in Lanza's outfit. We were all excited at the time. Loansharking and pimping only pay so much. Our activities selling things in back allies or off the back of a truck were pinched in their own ways. Coke though, that had real possibility. People had gotten rich selling it. It was the 80's and from the suits in a glass tower to a thug on the street, everyone wanted some.

Anyway, Jim had jumped at the chance. Our whole crew had been behind him, and all of us were looking forward to more, business. So, to Columbia, he went with Mustache and Johnny. We had been discussing how much better things would be, all the nice things we would buy, all the birds we would shag, when we got the news. Apparently, some rebels had come to the jungle town Jim was at. They had murdered and burned half the village, chasing the locals into the jungle. Mustache's body was recovered and was being sent back to the States. They thought they had found Johnny too, or what was left of him, no one could be sure. Whatever mess it was, flew in a box next to Mustache for burial. Jim's body wasn't found, but he was declared dead. The Colombian government had no way to be sure, but those small jungle towns meant nothing to them. It was assumed he had died and was rotting somewhere in the greenery. It was a dark day.

So, there we were, a bunch of micks mostly, without a leader. Jim was the guy Lanza trusted out of our crew. With him gone, our prospects in the city were limited and possibly short term. I tried to fill Jim's shoes, but Lanza just didn't respect me the way he did Jim. At first, he only told me to send him his cut, but within a week or two, he upped his percentage. Our guys were doing the same work, but we kept less. Crispy, one of our guys, was a 2nd or 3rd cousin to Lanza. He was part mick, part wop, smaller than most but with the biggest attitude. His name was Alberto, but everyone just called him Crispy on account of him having burned his eyebrows off during an insurance job. He went to talk to Lanza on our behalf. We hoped that since they were related, Lanza might go easy on him.

Unfortunately for us, Crispy had other ideas. He ended up taking over Johnny Vaccaro's crew and Lanza let it be known that we had to answer to the little bastard as well. The writing was on the wall, and even though we were only a few weeks past Jim's death, Crispy started taking more for himself and Vaccaro's boys. He still came to Molloy's once in a while, but it wasn't out of friendship. He put on a show that we were all in the same crew and that it was just bigger now, but when the chips fell, he came out the winner.

And so it went for a few weeks. Things getting worse, money getting tighter, tensions starting to rise. We talked about it when Crispy wasn't around. Some of the guys started talking about going elsewhere, Chicago, or Philly, or maybe even leaving the life. A couple of our guys hired on with Mustache's old crew. His boys were mostly enforcers, but they had their own rackets down by The Wharf too. Fishing companies and other businesses along the piers were perfect for cleaning money. Even with Mustache dead, they weren't going anywhere. The shops were too important.

It had been a rough couple of months. But then the call came in. I was working the bar at Molloy's and when the phone rang, I grabbed it while serving some locals a couple of beers.

"Jakey, how you doin' bro?" I froze as I heard Jim's voice.

"Holy shit, Jim, is that you? For real?" The feelings of relief, and gratitude, and of a weight being lifted were almost too much to describe.

"For real. I'd ask why you aren't picking me up, but I guess you thought I was dead huh?"

"Yeah Jimmy, you're dead. Where the hell are you?" My hands were shaking. The boys heard me talking and started coming my way.

"SFO. I just got off the plane. Get the boys together. I'll grab a cab and be there in 20, maybe 30." And he hung up. I guess the look on my face said it all. Tommy, "Red", because of his red socks, reached out and squeezed my shoulder. "That really Jimmy?" one of the boys asked. I wasn't sure which one, I was too stunned. I just nodded.

Chapter 2

Homecoming

It was one of those gray San Francisco days where the mist hung everywhere. It cloaked the streets and buildings, dampening sound, and giving the city a smaller, almost safer feel. The wind was kicking up and before long rain started to fall through the mist. Eventually, the wind began to clear the fog that hung at street level and we just had the soft pitter-patter of light rain. As the sky darkened the rain became heavier, falling in torrents that alternated with a light drizzle. First heavy wind, then a loud rush as a drenching downpour hit the streets, cars, and people. Then the lighter sound. The overcast sky alternating between elemental violence and natural peace. People bustled back and forth, hunching themselves into the wind. Some had umbrellas or hats they shielded their faces with. This overcast darkness and rhythmic rain was common to the Bay Area.

It was during one of the violent torrents that I saw the yellow and black checker pull up in front of Molloy's. My breath caught. I had spent the last half hour wondering if I had really heard Jim's voice on the phone. A waterfall of rain was drenching the street in front of us. But in a few seconds, there he stood having exited the taxi. The car rolled off as Jim walked purposefully towards the bar door. I was out from behind the counter in a flash, and the rest of the boys had started to get out of their chairs. There he was, walking, head high as the rain poured down, eyes bright, and he nodded at us with a slight smile.

Jim beat me to the door and pushed it open as he walked in. "Jakey!!" He said and gave me a big hug. But the rest of the boys were there too, and all were happy to clap him on the shoulder or shake his hand or offer him a drink.

"What the hell Jim?" Red asked.

"Rebels couldn't keep you down could they Jimmy?" Marty.

"Glad to have you back Jimmy." Old Man Stark said.

"Whiskey's all around!!" Cried another voice.

In their excitement, the boys spoke over one another, greeting Jim, then talking to the guys next to them. There were a few minutes of conversation and insults back and forth, as guys who have spent too many years together usually resort to. Jim was in his element, with his crew, and he gave insults as good as he got them. "You smell like jungle rot Jim". "Oh yeah, still better than your aftershave Old Man." Or "You hiding out and banging Columbian salsa boss?" "Not as hard as I hammered your mom Red". And the like, typical guy crap.

Knowing Jim and I would catch up later, I backed off and let the rest of the crew have at him. It was then that I noticed his hair was dry, and there was barely any dampness on the shoulders of his jacket. There was a strength about him, a purpose. Now don't get me wrong, Jim had always had purpose, ambition. He'd always been charismatic and been one of those people whose eyes seemed to have a physical force. It was almost as if when they looked at you, you felt pushed backward or caught in their grip. But at the back of my mind, I knew something was different.

I might have paid more attention, but if you remember, I said "almost everyone" was glad to see Jim. See the thing was, Crispy was there that night. He had come by to give us marching orders and to throw his weight around a bit. Since he had taken over, he had started to be a real asshole to the Old Man.

Old Man Stark was one of those older guys you didn't fuck with. He was a bit past sixty, but he'd been in the game for a long time, and he was strong. You know the type. You see an old guy, and you immediately discount him, dismiss him. But every once in awhile, you come across some crusty, aged bastard whose handshake is like iron, their shoulders broad, the look in their eyes dauntless. You know that son of a bitch is not to be trifled with. Old Man Stark was like that. Crispy didn't like him on account that they crossed swords some years back. Crispy had thought to push the limits with this old man. He dismissed him like you should never do to a guy like Stark. In the end, the Old Man had beaten the crap out of Alberto in the alley behind Molloy's.

Most of us spent a few months sticking it to Crispy after that, mostly because we knew better than to mess with Stark. The shame never left, however. I guess that's what happens when you're a twenty-something, arrogant hothead, and you get your ass handed to you by a grandpa, a non-entity. The reality was, there was no shame in getting beat to shit by a guy like the Old Man. The only one in our crew who had a chance was Jim, and they never pushed each other. But Crispy just never let it go.

So there he was before Jim arrived giving Stark the business. The Old Man was told to act as a bag boy or other stupid crap for the numbers gig that junior guys were supposed to do. Stark took it though. He needed the money. Stark was a loyal man, loyal to the last. He had a daughter somewhere, and even though they never talked, he still sent her some of his earnings. Besides, with Lanza backing Crispy, well, it wouldn't have been good for him if he repeated the back alley beating from years before.

Knowing this, I decided to keep an eye on Crispy. He was a liar and a thief, but he was only good at being a thief. He tried to put on a show of being happy Jim was back, but you could see the strained smile, the twitch at the edge of his mouth. I figured right then and there that unless Jim could talk some sense into Lanza, things would keep going South, only faster.

The next bit or so Crispy sat with Jim and the boys and had a couple of drinks. Our leader was telling us how he had run into the jungle after being shot. He had spent a few weeks near death in some native hut somewhere. He had a hole in his leg and nearly bled out, or so he thought. After running into the jungle, he had passed out, only to wake up he didn't know how long after, in some hut he didn't know where. His leg had been bandaged with a weird jungle concoction that smelled horrible. He was in and out, fevered for a while. It had to have been at least a couple of weeks. After that, he spent some time limping around this new village, full of rain forest natives deep in the Choco jungle.

Choco was the part of the jungle most people don't go to. It's perfect for getting a deal done, but for the same reason, most people don't go there. Colombian rebels are vicious, and if you're not dealing with them, well, you're meat. Jimmy, Mustache, and Johnny had been dealing with the wrong rebel group and paid the price.

I bused the table and got more drinks for everyone, sitting with the group intermittently. Someone else could have done it, but I wanted to keep an eye on Crispy. He made it about 45 minutes, tension building in his shoulders, face getting tired of faking a smile. Eventually, it was too much and I watched him get up, handing Stark an envelope with his work. He then shook Jim's hand and headed out. He didn't notice me watching, and the dark look on his face told me everything I needed to know.

He went out into the rain. It was light at the time with just a trace of the San Francisco fog lingering. As he walked it appeared he was looking back to the bar, checking to see if anyone was watching. I saw him duck into a payphone down the block and almost out of view. Right then Jim's table erupted in laughter from too many drunk micks.

"Show us the bullet hole Jim, or else I'm going to think you were getting with some Colombian pussy instead of working!" Yelled a drunk and red-faced Stitch.

"Drop my pants for you Stitch? At the table? You going queer on me man?" Was the reply followed by a round of laughter.

I had looked at the table when it got so loud. When I looked back to the booth, Crispy was gone. Thinking on it, though, I was worried. Jim's oddities weren't even a memory. I was too focused on how Crispy had behaved. I knew for sure that not everyone was happy Jim was back.

Chapter 3

My Apartment

Much later that night, Jim and I sat in my apartment throwing back glasses of bourbon. I had stayed mostly dry while keeping an eye on Crispy and out of nervousness kept it to light drinking the rest of the night. After getting home it was time to catch up. Jim didn't seem the worse for wear and was trading shot for shot with me as we damaged the bottle. We spent some time together just joking and talking, like when we were kids.

He had taken his jacket and shirt off and sat in his slacks and a wife beater. He wore a new necklace, a light blue stone wrapped in copper wire on a leather thong. He reached up and fingered it absently.

"Get that from one of the Colombian girls Jim?" I asked.

"Heh, you know it." He smiled, then, "Actually from the old bastard who took care of me after I got shot. He gave it to me when he was changing my bandage. Kept saying suerte, suerte and nodding his head. It wasn't until I was back in Bogota that I found out the word meant luck. The guy gave me a good luck charm. It's probably what saved me. Lord knows it couldn't have been the crap he put on my leg."

We knocked a couple more shots back. It had been a while and I decided to let him know the trouble our crew was in. "We're having difficulties with Crispy, Jim. Lanza put him in charge of Vaccaro's crew. Some of Mustache's guys are working with him too. He's been squeezing us."

We discussed the way Crispy had been changing the percentages, how some of our guys had moved on to The Wharf or elsewhere, and how Crispy was using his new position to mess with the guys he had had friction with. All the while we kept drinking.

"I wondered what was up. Was that envelope he gave Stark some rookie numbers gig?" I nodded and he continued, "Figures, he wants to stick it to the Old Man. Dumbass. I'll talk to Lanza tomorrow."

"Whatcha gonna say bro?" The shots had gotten to my brain and I was slurring my words.

He smiled big, "I got the deal done in Colombia. The powder arrives in a few weeks." He knocked another shot back and looked at the empty glass and shook his head. " I found another supplier. That ought to buy us something with The Big Guy."

I started to laugh a bit as I drifted off into unconsciousness. The feeling that things were going to get better played across my mind. How one man could hold so much power, I never had understood. With one phone call and one cab ride, he had taken us from a dark, cornered existence to potential riches.

I vaguely remembered Jim downing what was left of the bottle and then swearing. But I couldn't be sure. Then I was out.

Chapter 4

Lanza

I dreamed that night.

I was on a nameless beach, looking out onto The Ocean. The water was deep and still, smooth as glass. The sky was gray and formless, almost nothing. In the distance to the West, a darkness grew, coalesced, and congealed brackish amid the sky and water. To the East, a brilliant light rose to answer it. I turned to face the light as I knew the black was too much to bear. From the brightness, I saw a man striding across the water, purposefully but unhurried. He walked calmly and the water slightly stirred with his footsteps. As he approached me, he raised his hands to the sky. A bolt of blue lightning leaped from his outstretched arms. Endless sparks and bolts poured forth from the man, filling the sky reflecting brilliant blue in the water. As the electricity cascaded from horizon to horizon a great thunder resonated and was followed by the wind. He continued his advance and as his arms dropped, the lightning in the heavens subsided. But the sky was different now. It was not a shapeless gray, but a new sky with the Sun, Moon, and Stars.

And still, he strode towards me.

I could not tear my eyes away for it was Jim. At least I thought so at first. As he got closer, I could see it wasn't him. It looked like Jim, but his eyes were different. Something ancient lived inside them. Blue fire and brilliant gold light poured from his eyes and wreathed his head. He opened his mouth to speak and I could not understand, it was like a great horn was sounding. The words were important but beyond my ability to comprehend. I only heard a horn. His eyes swept over me as he turned to face the darkness.

The black was not gone. It had grown and begun devouring portions of the sea and sky. He strode past me into the black part of the world still speaking, light and fire emanating from his eyes and mouth, and I could only hear the sound of a horn, like a magnificent trumpet. The wind howled.

I shot up in bed still hearing the sound. Covered in sweat, the sheets were stuck to me. I could have sworn the man stood at the foot of my bed, blue light coming from his eyes. Then I realized it was one of those times when you are half asleep and cannot tell dreams from reality. Jim stood at the foot of my bed wearing my best Armani. There was no light or fire in his eyes, nothing ancient, just Jim's blue eyes.

"I hope you don't mind me wearing your suit. Need to look respectable when talking to the big guy." Jim said retrieving some stuff from the bathroom. "I saw the boxes labeled with my name. I'll go through them later and get my clothes. I guess you cleared out my apartment when you heard I died. Hopefully, you didn't toss any of the good stuff."

The truth was that he looked better in that suit than I did. We were nearly the same size, but he was just a bit stockier than me. The suit fit almost perfectly, if a bit tighter around his arms and shoulders, his broader muscles hinted at behind the black herringbone. "Nah, you look good in it. Let me get ready, I'm going with you."

I heard him start the coffee maker as I slipped into the shower. After I dressed, we shared a cup of joe, and chatted about his game plan. The empty bourbon bottle in the trash was a testament to how much we had the night before. I wondered at how alert he looked. After a long day of travel and a longer night of throwing back drinks, you'd expect him to be wrecked. Not Jim, though. He was bright-eyed and radiated a sense of calm energy. His black hair and blue eyes accented a deliberate speech as he laid out his plans.

After finishing the coffee, we jumped into my gray-blue Buick and headed to Molloy's. There we picked up some iron and hung with the guys for a bit. Jim told them he would square things with Lanza and assured them we would be back to our old crew shortly.

After a couple of hours with the guys, we headed out of San Francisco. Lanza was at one of his homes outside of the city, in Mill Valley. We crossed the Golden Gate into Marin. It was a glorious day, one that gave the area the name Golden Gate. The sun reflected brilliant gold across the deep blue water. It created a view of a golden mirror surrounded by sapphire waves. In the distance, you could see a wall of fog coming in. It too is one of those unique features of the Bay Area. These fog banks move across the water and land like a gray barrier. Its wisps and tendrils making one feel like it was almost alive. In minutes the bank could envelop the land turning a bright day into a muted, darker existence. Below the bridge, we could see people on their sailboards.

I couldn't help but remember my dream. I saw Jim, or the not-Jim, walking out of the light, across the waves towards me. The fog even reminded me of the growing darkness. The dream had not faded as they often do. It was fresh in my mind, as real as the car we were in. I shook my head slightly and departed my reverie, but I couldn't shake the feeling that the vision had meant something.

We drove into the quiet hills of Mill Valley. It was a small town with a hippy, bohemian culture. Houses were nestled into nice, wooded areas up and down the foothills. One of the town's greatest features was that it sported some giant redwood trees.

When we arrived at Lanza's compound, the gates were open. One of his bruisers stood watch at the gate and waved us in. After pulling up into the rounder beside the front door, we were searched and relieved of our weapons, then shown in. Walking through the house, we could see the comfortable life Lanza's Family had netted him. Expensive antique furniture filled the home, and there were all the latest housing upgrades. He was having some food out on the deck with views of the town below. Crispy was already seated there. A couple of Mustache's guys, now Crispy's guys, stood watch at a polite distance from the table.

Lanza smiled a big smile and waved us into a couple of chairs. "Jakey! Good to see you. And Jimmy, glad you're back from the dead!"

James Lanza was an old man by this time. He was in his eighties, but he was healthy. He had taken over the Mob Family in the early 60's and even had his picture on the front of LIFE magazine listing him as the crime boss of San Francisco. Overall, he had kept the Family small since his ascension. There weren't many made men. He kept it that way, only making men he had the utmost trust in. This was to limit the number of informants that might sing against him in case the Feds took a look at the family business. Lanza had reached out and worked with other people in the life, always careful to keep them at a distance. That was why our crew, Jim's boys, a bunch of dirty micks, were by extension in Lanza's network. In fact, it was usually only Jim that met with him, but I had become the contact when Jim disappeared into the rain forest.

A low-level grunt came out from the house and took our drink and sandwich orders, then went back in. We made small talk, nothing related to business until he had returned with our food and one of the torpedoes closed the door to the deck after he left.

When we were alone, Lanza started the conversation. "Jimmy my boy, we're glad you're back. Losing Mustache and Johnny was bad enough. We're glad we didn't lose all three of you."

"Good to see you too boss. I just wanted to touch base and let you know I'm back." Jim replied.

"Great, so what can I do for you?"

Jim looked at Lanza and then Crispy, then back to Lanza. "Well, I want things back the way they were. You raised our percentage and Crispy here has been taking extra too. A couple of my boys went to the wharf. So, we're a little short on guys, working harder, and keeping less."

"I needed to pay some guys to help keep up your business, you know Jimmy. I still might have to if you are short."

Jim shook his head. "We're good. I will take care of things that need taking care of. I always have."

At that Lanza nodded. "Yes, you have my boy. Yes, you have. Alright, I will think it over. What have you got for me?"

"I completed the deal in Colombia. Our first shipment lands in three weeks. There should be plenty to go around. I dealt with a man named General Lopez, one of the rebels in the jungle. He has plenty of product and had just finished killing our other contact down there. He's eager to be involved with us."

"You dealt with the man who killed my people?" Lanza said in surprise.

"There was nothing else to do. I couldn't take revenge, he has too many people and besides, what would that have done for business? Nothing. He didn't even know who he was killing besides his rivals."

Lanza thought for a bit, and then "I like the ambition, Jimmy. Business first, always. Very well, good work. I will let you know on the other stuff. Crispy here will touch base with you on details."

It was a clear dismissal, also, with that one phrase he had placed Crispy between Jim and himself. On the surface, the conversation had gone pretty well, but that one act was not good for our crew. There was now a distance between Jim and Lanza that hadn't existed before.

Before leaving we had a final toast with some good brandy. We drained crystal glasses of the amber liquid, got up and headed out shaking hands on the way. After collecting our iron, we jumped in the car and headed back into the city, crossing the Golden Gate as we had on the way out. The fog had rolled in most of the way and the day was taking on a darker cast.

Later on, Jim and Crispy would talk details by phone. Jim had spent nearly a million dollars of ours and the family's money on the shipment coming in. It was a good bit of product and as usual, it would come in on one of the fishing boats out of the wharf.

Chapter 5
The Wharf

Fisherman's Wharf is a well-known tourist spot in the city. People come from all over San Francisco and Marin County, even the country to head down to The Wharf. There are old ships set up as museums. You can get helicopter tours or catch ferries across the bay. Alcatraz tours start on boats off one of the piers. Alcatraz, that old and decommissioned prison, is a big tourist spot. A few movies have been made about it. Along the Wharf piers, there are also lots of shops and restaurants and many other things for tourists with a bit of loose change to spend on. It's iconic.

What few people know is that the Wharf was started by Francesco Lanza, or Frank as he was known. That's right, Frank Lanza, James Lanza's dad, and the then leading founder of the San Francisco mob. A corrupt, gang leading, numbers running, whore managing, protection racket starting (and a whole lot of other things) wop by the name of Frank Lanza started The Wharf. I'll bet you didn't know that, did you? It was the 1930's and he fought bloody, street-level gang wars with other greasy wops over the territory. In fact, The Lanza family rose after murdering their rival Luigi Malvese in 1932. That's when they took de facto control of San Francisco organized crime. Mobsters started a nationally known tourist destination. Crazy right?

Anyway, I guess the history isn't that important, except that James Lanza still controlled The Wharf. Things had changed, armed thugs didn't walk around busting heads. But the thing is, The Wharf was a source of money and money cleaning for The Family. It was maybe harder to spot in the '80s, but everyone down there paid their dues one way or the other to Lanza.

And our new shipment was coming from Colombia, due to be smuggled in through Pacific Crab, a business on a pier. And now, with Mustache gone, Crispy controlled The Wharf for Lanza. So, you can see where I'm going with this, or where it was headed one way or the other. Sure, Lanza himself could have stopped it, but that wasn't in the cards. And the Wharf itself, Fisherman's Wharf, would be at the center of bloody conflict, gangland-style.

Chapter 6

The Drumbeat of War

We didn't know it at the time, of course. A couple days after our meeting, Jim got a call from Crispy. Lanza had agreed to return us to our old percentages, but Crispy was in charge of the Wharf. He said we were going to have to renegotiate the terms of the Colombian deal. Lanza had said it was between Jim and Crispy, and with Crispy controlling The Wharf, well, unfortunately, he held the upper hand.

We got our first clue that something was up when Crispy called. When San Francisco's finest in blue raided and shut down one of our book-making rackets, we knew we had our second. So here's the thing, rumor has it that Lanza was good friends with Joseph Alioto. Now Alioto had been the mayor of San Francisco a few years prior. Alioto denied the friendship, of course, but what we did know was that Lanza had connections with the police. There are usually some connections between the mob and government. Grease a police sergeant's palm here, make a political donation say to a mayor, and as long as things don't get out of hand, the authorities usually look the other way. For us micks, Lanza had always covered us when it came to the cops. He had the connections.

Our odds joint had been overlooked by police "protection" for years. Hell, we would even see a few cops in there from time to time placing bets. One sergeant was a regular, and his "winnings" were how we paid him. Jim had arranged the set up with Lanza awhile back. So, when the business got busted and shut down, we knew something was going wrong.

We were lucky. Our guy Stitch usually covered that joint. He was on his way back when he saw the black and whites. They were all over the place and the odds making crew was being taken out in handcuffs. The money, the books, everything was taken. I can tell you those books never saw the light of day, probably trashed in a can somewhere or ash in a barrel. There were more than a few pigs who had placed bets with us. At any rate, Stitch walked away before they could spot him. When he called to tell us, we found a hidey-hole for him in a hooker's apartment across town.

A day or so later Jim got another call from Crispy. He used the bust as a reason to strong-arm us. What he basically said was that the heat was on our operation, and because of that, he would need to handle the shipment coming in from Colombia. Of course, there would be additional fees for handling our business for us. When Jim and I ran the numbers, our crew would make less than they had put in. Crispy and Lanza would make all the profit plus some of our original stake. "It's the only way" Crispy had said, "it had to be done."

Jim and I knew instantly this was probably the opening act of a play to remove us from our own businesses. Crispy knew them all, and in his mind, he probably felt we were just taking money that could be his. Also, we weren't part of The Family. We were just micks working under the capo of San Francisco. We were disposable.

To head things off, Jim requested a meeting with Lanza himself. The boss ignored Jim's request. He just went silent. His other Family members would beg off on his behalf or simply tell Jim that it was between him and Crispy.

We knew then that we were fucked.

Chapter 7

The Troops

It was another stormy night when Jim came to Molloy's to tell the crew. It was wet and raining again. This time I noticed it, Jim was dry when he came in from the street. He pushed the door open and Red, Stark, Marty, and I got up to head for the back room.

Now one of the things about Jim is that he was a natural leader. He had that born charisma that some people seem to possess. It was the kind of charm that made people he didn't know want to get on his good side. When you had spent time around him, his manner was something that just created a sense of loyalty. I guess it could be described as a combination of wanting to make him happy while also believing you were more than you were when he was around. For people who didn't like him, or who he didn't get along with, his presence inspired fear.

Growing up I looked up to him. Because he was a couple years older, he was bigger than me too. I followed him around like a puppy dog when we were kids. Later on, in high school, I always tried to tag along with him. For the most part, he let me. I guess he liked me being around as a sidekick. Because he was always invited to the good parties, I would get to go. All the most popular girls liked his bad-boy image. We both had that persona, of course, coming from where we did. It worked for him much better than it did me. For years I wished I was him, and it did cause some problems. Fighting was a thing for us then, and he and I went at it many times. Usually, he was the winner. Once in a while, it was me. I took pride in those times. I still do. But when it came to other people, we always had each other's backs.

Anyway, when he walked in with that confidence, that presence, I almost didn't see he was dry. But see it I did and paused to grab Jim's arm as he went by me, "What's going on Jimmy?" I asked brushing his dry shoulder. "How the hell?" I had spoken in a low tone so none of the others could hear us.

Jim smiled patiently, knowing that I knew he had a secret. "We'll get to that, not tonight though." He nodded and pushed me towards the back.

Stitch was already back there staying out of sight. We needed him, but we also needed to make sure he wasn't taken in by the cops. So, we all gathered in that room, doors closed. There was only a single light bulb hanging from a wire in the center of the room. Smoke from a couple guys smoking hung in the air. It was dark and gloomy, and the mood was tense.

Jim was calm but upbeat when he laid out the situation. Crispy was breathing down our necks. He was going to take our shipment. Lanza was content to watch how it played out between us and his crew. Crispy controlled The Wharf and Mustache's guys, so it seemed like he held the upper hand. Depending on how hard Crispy pushed and he was pushing hard, we would have a choice to make, bend over and take it in the ass, or go to war.

Near the end of the meeting, Stark grunted. "Well boss, whatcha gonna do? It's for sure certain he's trying to fuck us, take us out of our own place."

Again, that patient smile, and considering the odds we faced, a familiar confidence lit those blue eyes, "Well Old Man, I'm game for war if you are." His confidence was almost too much considering the situation, but it was genuine.

"Between Crispy, Mustache's, and Vaccaro's crew we're looking at 16 to 18 men. There's only 6 of us."

"Yep", Jim nodded, "They don't have enough."

There was worry on everyone's faces except Stark and Jim. I'm not ashamed to say it. It was on mine as well. I thought we were looking at shortened lifespans. Then the Old Man grunted again, "What the hell, I'm sick of that runt's shit anyways. Let's do it."

With that, the table burst into laughter. Jim's demeanor and leadership had steered us where he wanted us to go. A feeling of purpose settled over the guys. Knowing the odds were against us, our confidence still soared once we had chosen our path. A road may lead to ruin, but a man will walk it quickly once he's decided on his course.

Chapter 8

Our First Response

We got word from one of our pimps in Butchertown that a guy from Crispy's crew had stopped by. Now this guy, his name was "Bull" DeLano. He wasn't made, but he was a wop. He was also big, strong, and dumb. A bruiser from Mustache's crew, he was now doing what Crispy told him. And what Crispy had said was that our pimp, Goldfinger on account that he loved James bond, was to pay Bull from then on out.

If you know Butchertown, at least back then, the place was a dump. It was an industrial area, part residential homes, part industry, part meat rendering plant, which is where it got its name from. And at this time it still stank like a butcher shop. Our business was good there, though. Between all the blue-collar workers and the only working freight train that still came into SF, there were plenty of Johns that needed servicing. We sent out The Old Man.

I wasn't there, so I can't tell you all the details. But I do know this: As I said before, you don't fuck with a guy like Stark. Unfortunately, Bull was a younger version of Stark, even if he was dumber. It was probably a fight good enough for TV, but I can't give you a blow by blow as I didn't see it. Stark came out the winner with only a few broken ribs and a black eye. Bull went to the hospital with broken knees, orbital bone and wrist. Stark was making a statement to Crispy, Lanza, and anyone else who thought they might squeeze us.

Goldfinger would later that night recount a battle of titans. A brawl to end all brawls on the tracks near an abandoned home we used as a whorehouse. I can just imagine these two monsters punching it out in the gravel and dirt and stink of that place. Blood and teeth going, fog rolling in, and bystanders scurrying away as these two grunted and swung and kicked and grunted more. In the end, The Old Man came home with a bag of hard-won cash.

And Jim got another call from Crispy. It was on.

Chapter 9

Escalation

We were in Molloy's when the call came in. It was a couple of days after Stark and Bull tangled. I was in the back, grabbing a keg to replace one that had gone empty upfront. Red came in to get me with a sober look on his face. I followed him out of the back into the smoke-filled room. This was back when people weren't little girls who couldn't handle a hazy watering hole.

I loved Molloy's, the smell, the haze, the aging wooden tables, and even the broken people we called regulars. Bars are an interesting place. People of all kinds congregate there. You would have your college kids trying to get laid or after-hours worker drones trying to wash off the day with alcohol. The most common, of course, are the regulars. Often times they're broken people, drinking alone in a bar, looking for some sort of human connection. They are the most interesting. The stories of their lives, their triumphs, and the things that shattered them make for engaging people. Usually, they get too wasted to share their lives and end up drunk and alone, surrounded by people, and that makes them all the more lonely.

This evening as I was coming out of the back, I could see Jim on the phone. Molloy's was crowded with the previously mentioned patrons. A couple of our regulars were at the bar. One was nearly passed out already. In the corner sat a group of college kids "studying", books open and notes in front of them, forgotten as they flirted and tried to close the deal on the real reason they were there. At the bar and a couple of tables were different groups of well-dressed corporate do-nothings celebrating their successes or commiserating over their shitty bosses or whatever. Some of them were flirting too. More than one office romance or infidelity started with whiskey and a quickie in the bathrooms at Molloy's.

Our crew was at the largest table, a round table near the back, kicking back beers and chatting. Stark was seated, his black eye still evident, laughing and having a good time. Red sat back down, nursing his first beer. His back was to the wall so he could see the front. Since Bull and The Old man had tangled, we thought it was necessary to stay alert. That meant at least one of our crew was always sober, always watching. Tonight was Red's turn.

Now we didn't think anything would happen there, at the bar. It was pretty important for cleaning money and besides it was on a busy street and very public. Still, you never can be sure and we were concerned that something might happen. The cops had raided one of our bookies after all.

As I approached Jim, I could hear his voice calm but with an edge. "No, Crispy, that's not final. Those businesses are ours as is the shipment coming in. We will continue to operate AND we will get that shipment. Don't get in our way. Lanza will get his share, but if you fuck with us, well I think you'll have a bigger problem than you realize." With that, he hung up the phone.

He smiled at me reassuringly and squeezed my shoulder, "Looks like it's on." From the little I heard it sounded like he had declared war on Crispy and possibly the entire Lanza Family. Here's the thing, the mob doesn't back down. If they tell another crook something, they mean it. The only thing that stops them is force, blood, bullets, or whatever can break them or be shown to break them. I knew that if we didn't back down, or even if we did, we were likely dead. Jim had as much as drawn a line in the sand and dared Crispy, and through him Lanza, to cross it.

See the thing is, we knew Crispy wouldn't take a run at our businesses without approval from above. The mere fact that he had dared to tell Jim as much meant one of two things, either he had gone rogue against Lanza's wishes, or that Lanza had sanctioned the move. Crispy was an uppity little bastard but not so uppity as to go against the head of San Francisco. That phone call had brought our worst fears out. Lanza had given Crispy the green light.

You might know that the San Francisco mob was small, possibly the smallest in the country. It was often said that mobsters went to SF to retire or lay low. The Lanza Family had kept it this way for decades. It was even smaller under James Lanza. He had spent the better part of twenty years keeping strict control over who was made and who was just a lackey. He was worried about someone turning rat with the FBI or some other law enforcement office. As a result, San Francisco was pretty peaceful as far as mafia violence went. He usually kept it peaceful between us micks, the triads, and all the other assorted gangs.

Well, I guess that's not entirely true. The bangers and gooks weren't easy to tame, but they were low-level thugs as far as things went, so when they got out of hand The Family wasn't in danger.

Unfortunately for us, that's not how things always were. Like all cities, San Francisco had its share of mob violence. There was a period of time where four separate bosses for the Lanza family were whacked in succession. That time ended with James Lanza at the head of The Family his father had started. Even during peaceful times, the occasional hit would be authorized. It was usually done to keep SF quiet. Lanza would tell some torpedo to get out of the city because he was bringing too much heat. If said torpedo didn't leave, he would get whacked. More than one son of a bitch was found dead in the trunk of an old car as a result. Look it up. There's a case or two that make San Francisco famous for it. We might have been a part of that on occasion. Hell, we might even have been part of murders you can easily lookup. Of course, I'll leave that research to you.

Anyway, we knew with this final phone call things had just gotten ugly. The peace in the city was broken, Crispy was gunning for us, and the only thing that would stop the carnage now was if one side or the other was gone. Our crew, descendants at least in spirit, of the old K&A gang from a hundred years prior, had been loyal to Lanza, had made him and his Family money for decades. The truth was, though, that didn't mean shit. Crispy had decided to take our business and Lanza was backing him. Of all the syndicates in the city, we were the only ones that had become orphans. Besides our crew, we had no help, no backup, no safe shelter. We were all destined to end up in the trunk of said car or some other equally, deadly location.

The guys sobered up quickly that night. We closed Molloy's early, put the drinks away, and talked about our next move. It was about two and a half weeks before our shipment would come in from Colombia. We aimed to be there to get it. In the meantime, we knew we had a fight on our hands, the fight of our lives, a fight for our lives.

Jim didn't talk about it like that, though. To him, it was an opportunity. Lanza had turned his back on us, betrayed us. Jim thought that was a good thing. No more percentages and no more rules. He started laying out plans not just to protect our business but to take more. The first thing was that no one was to go out alone. We paired up, me and Jim, Stark and Stitch, Red and Marty. The next thing was as of that night our weekly payments to Lanza stopped. As far as Jim was concerned the old, wop bastard could go fuck himself. The third was that we needed to recruit some more guys. We spent some time discussing who some of the up and comers in our businesses were. This was mostly about the vicious kids, those too ambitious or stupid to back down from a fight. We needed thugs, torpedoes, muscle. Finally, we decided on a target. We weren't just going to sit back and protect what was ours. We were going to take what was theirs.

Chapter 10
Offense

The first thing we did was send Red and Marty to deal with a bag man for Crispy. It was a minor attack, really, but according to Jim, it was to get Crispy's attention. One of Vaccaro's crew collected a take from the triads in Chinatown. In San Francisco, there are actually four different China Towns. That's another detail most people don't know. They think there's only one. There are chinks all over the city. When you hear the name Chinatown you generally think of the first one, the biggest one, the tourist trap. That one is known because more people visit it than even the Golden Gate. The Chinese are an interesting lot, keeping to themselves for the most part. They are intensely loyal inside their circles, and Chinatown is no different. The Chinese would rather eat at a restaurant owned by one of their own, or shop at a store, or do just about anything rather than deal with outsiders. Hell, they'll even go to a Chinese doctor, knowing that the doctor is mediocre, rather than go to a white doctor with a good reputation.

The Chinatown we were interested in was smaller and in the Sunset district. Sunset is a big neighborhood, the largest in San Francisco. All sorts of people live there, and the triads had more than one whorehouse masquerading as a massage parlor. As with much of the crime in the city, those hookers were protected by Lanza's connections with the cops.

For most of the businesses in the city, a bag man would go once a week to collect Lanza's due. In the case of the Sunset district, it had been in Vaccaro's area, now Crispy's. Red and Marty were there at dusk, waiting. A low-level thug working for the little runt was making his bones, working the district. He was no match for our two guys. As he was leaving the last parlor, they slid up behind him and put a gun in his back. A short walk later and they were in his car, taking the bags collected from the different businesses in Sunset. It was easy as pie.

They could have left it there if they wanted, but they didn't. They drove the poor bastard to an empty lot and beat the crap out of him. He was left lying by his car, beat, not as bad as some, but bad nonetheless. We heard he ran from the city a day or two later. In truth, the beating probably saved him from something worse once Crispy got him. I hope he got out of the life after he ran. If not, at least he got out of the war that came soon after.

Meanwhile, across town, Jim and I were setting up for the bigger heist. We had corralled four guys from the lower ranks of our businesses. Their names don't matter. They were just some of the meaner guys, guys angry enough or desperate enough to get into the life in the first place, but angrier and more desperate than most. So, they made good muscle.

Our target was a seafood restaurant near The Wharf. It was a nice place, with tourists and a higher-end customer. It also had gambling in the basement. Decades ago, the lower level had been a speakeasy. Now it featured card games and even a roulette table.

By the time we arrived, we expected Lanza or Crispy had heard about the attack in Chinatown. It was probable that they had sent some of their guys to find the wounded bag man. That's what Jim wanted, their resources spread out.

The restaurant sat on a small, side street about a block up from The Wharf. It was one of those cozier locations that hide in tourist areas. Small, boutique shops and places to eat that cater to the more knowledgeable higher-ups in the city and tourists in the know. More exotic wares, more expensive food meant for a more elite clientele.

We went in the back. Like many restaurants, it had a regular inner door with an outer metal security gate used by busboys or other waitstaff during business hours. We waited on either side of the door in nondescript clothes with ski masks on until a worker in a white coat came out carrying trash. One of our thugs put a gun to his head and pushed him back inside. We followed.

The thug in the lead, quietly got the kitchen staff up against the wall, while two more of our guys went into the dining room. We heard them yelling at the staff and customers as they set about robbing everyone blind. There was one shout and I heard a crunch as someone got knocked down into a table or chair, and the dining room went quiet except for the shouted instructions from our criminal underlings.

Through a door in the kitchen, there was a staircase into the basement where our real target was. Jim, I, and the last bruiser headed down while the other three took care of the top. At the bottom of the stairs was a heavy wooden door, locked and barred from the inside. It had one of those sliding panels that would open so people could talk through the door. It was used so the guard inside could get the password from those wanting to gamble. Only people who knew the right word or phrase would be allowed entry. Jim had told me he had the password and he knocked on the door. As the panel started to slide open, Jim, who was in the lead, stepped back and kicked that door. There was an incredible crash as the door and frame broke inward onto the guard. I could see him flailing as he went down with the mass of smashed door landing on top. A metal crossbar bent from the force skittered across the floor. I was in shock. No one, not even Stark was that strong.

"What the fuck?" I couldn't help but blurt out.

"I told you I knew the password." Jim laughed as he stepped through the door. "Come on. Let's get this done."

Dumbfounded, I followed him in. Passing into the rooms behind, I checked to make sure our thug was close. He was, and his eyes were wide in astonishment as he surveyed the wreckage of the door. I nodded in approval as even in shock, he had the wherewithal to kick the downed guard in the head putting him out.

Two more guards came at us, one from either side drawing weapons. I was too quick for the one on the right, closing the distance and racking him across the face with my pistol. He went down in a spray of red and the sound of his nose breaking. I heard a thud and turned to see the other guard sliding down the wall, a smear of blood from the back of his head where it had impacted. Jim briefly stood over him before turning and heading into the gambling room. We followed.

Inside were the regular gaming tables, roulette, poker, blackjack, and a few others I didn't recognize. There were plenty of people there all looking up in surprise. A pit boss who doubled as an enforcer was already heading towards us but went down when Jim shot him in the gut. The remaining two guards put up their hands as us two lackeys disarmed them and put them face down. At least one could see a broken guard in the outer room and thought it wiser to live than to fight.

"Ladies and gentlemen", Jim yelled to the crowd, "do what we ask, and no one else will get hurt. We're just here for the money, but if you fuck with us, well..." He let the last word hang as he gestured to the guy on the ground bleeding out from his torso. And he finished with "Everyone's hands up!". Arms around the room immediately raised to the sky.

I'm not proud of this next part. His name was Luca DiAmadeo. He was actually a pretty nice guy, at least as mobsters go. A college graduate and an accountant, he'd been made by Lanza shortly after he got out of college. He'd been made with a minimum of violence. Some of the tougher guys in San Francisco talked shit on him behind his back. He was a pencil pusher they said. He was a nerd. And that was true. He rose through the ranks because he was loyal to Lanza, his family was connected to The Family by blood, and because he was great at cleaning money. He also had a wife and a couple of kids. I shot him in the face.

He was behind the final door, in the room with all the mob's gambling cash. I unlocked it with keys taken from the guard I had put on the ground. As I opened the door, a shot rang out, missing me by a couple of inches. Luca was crouched behind his desk at the back of the room aiming at the door with only his gun, hands and head visible. I jumped left into the room firing back at him as he opened up on me. One of his strays hit a gambler in the back. I don't know which shot hit Luca, only that as I charged towards his desk firing, hearing his bullets strike the wall behind me, I saw a blossom of red and brown and bone spray up against the wall and he flopped back. As I finished coming round the desk I saw him lying there, a hole in his cheek and the back of his open head seeping red blood and the clear milk of spinal fluid into a pool.

Shaking, I opened the bag I had brought and started loading it with money from around the room. There was a lot there. Being in the business, we had a good idea of what days there would be a good amount of cash in the back. We got almost all of it, only leaving the stuff covered in death. Jim and our torpedo looted the gambling room while I was in the back and the guys upstairs cleaned out the restaurant. There was soundproofing downstairs, but it wasn't enough to mute the gunfire and we heard sirens headed in our direction as the six of us went out the way we had come in. We split up into twos and followed different routes through the city. Our masks and jackets found their way into dumpster fires or public trashcans. All our guns would go into the bay a few hours later.

Jim's plan worked well. Because the restaurant had been robbed, and because a couple people had been shot, the cops had to clear the place out. Lanza's contacts couldn't save the gambling spot. The robbery was too public. Now mind you, we didn't intend to shoot anyone but it's always a possibility with something like that. Also, it didn't hurt our plan to have some bodies needing to be cleaned up there. The whole thing made the Chronicle front page the next day.

We all met up later at Goldfinger's whorehouse in Butchertown. The six of us, and our four new thugs all crashed there for the night. We split the money up not worrying about if we should spend it or not. There was no way that Lanza wouldn't blame us, even if the cops didn't. Jim and I put ours into a bank deposit box and hid the key. I can't tell you what the other guys did with their cuts. We did get a lot though, and that was just cash. There was plenty of jewelry to go around, but we didn't have time to get to a pawn shop or some other way to sell it, so that went into the bank too. Jim bought all the guys a girl that night, except me. I didn't want any part of that. The pimp had a tendency to leave bruises and scars on the girls from his rings. Instead, Jim and I spent the night keeping watch. We knew that Lanza would need vengeance.

Chapter 11

Reprisal

For the next couple of days, we went our separate ways. We stayed in pairs, of course, but we scattered for a bit, keeping in touch by phone. Red and Marty made it to Molloy's, but they went in through the back. They handled a bit of business there but spotted one of Crispy's bruisers watching the place from a half-block away. The guy was sitting in his car, throwing the occasional cigarette butt onto the street and drinking what looked to be a shitty canned beer. They stayed out of sight until Red decided to take matters into his own hands.

Red was a pretty good-looking guy, brown hair, and brown eyes. He kept his hair a little long, and in the San Francisco wind, it was always messy. He was on the smaller side, but even so, he was great with the ladies and always had been. He was also a bit of a peacock, wearing nice clothes with some sort of flare, like a loud tie pin or a red handkerchief in the pocket. We called him Red because he always wore red socks. It was his signature peacock feather. But besides being a player, Red had scars. Red had grown up in one of the poorer parts of Chicago. At the age of 12, his dad, a drunken bastard, sent Red to live with his uncle in San Francisco. Apparently, the uncle was no peach either, but it was still better than Chicago. Then said uncle died when our friend was 14. Rather than get put into the system, he basically ran away and raised himself on the streets. This is how we met him. This was the beginning of the formation of our crew. Red made his way for a good 10 to 15 years fighting, mugging people, selling stolen goods, and boosting car stereos or the cars themselves and then selling them to chop shops. In fact, he got really good at it. As part of our crew, he was in charge of a chop shop just outside of Chinatown. Most low-level street thieves knew they could turn a decent car into that garage for a buck. The car would become parts in a matter of hours.

Red still knew how to steal cars. He was near the top of our food chain, so he never did it anymore, but he knew how. At Molloy's, he grabbed a screwdriver and headed out the back. Apparently, there was one of those old white Dodge Ram vans, you know, the ones without windows. We call them murder vans because you can't see what's going on inside. Well, Red just walked right up to that van, rammed his screwdriver into the door lock and opened it. He had the wires out and that van fired up in less than a minute. The way Marty told it, Red drove that van around the block, threw it in reverse and backed up repeatedly into the Lincoln the previously mentioned bruiser was sitting in. Pull forward, back up into the Lincoln, pull forward, back up into the Lincoln. Crispy's guy was screaming at first, trying to get out the passenger side of the car. He might have pulled a gun and gotten a shot off, Marty wasn't sure. The car ended up on its side with the crumpled back of the van wedged into the underbelly.

Red hopped out of that van and strolled down the street cool as could be. At first people stared at him, but as he turned the corner, he faded into the crowd. Marty picked him up a block farther up, and the two headed to a shitty hotel in Oakland.

Across town, Jim and I were setting up an ambush. Goldfinger had gotten a call from Crispy that Chuck "The Hammer" was swinging by to pick up Lanza's take on the operation in Butchertown. It was dusk, but already pretty dark as the sky was covered in thick, gray clouds. The two of us set up behind a dumpster in an alley partway down the block. Then the rain started.

I pulled my coat in tight and hugged the wall hoping to get some shelter from the overhang on the brick building we were up against. Jim just stood there. I marveled again at how he didn't squint when the water started pouring heavily from the sky. A light steam rising from broad shoulders could be seen as the water hit his jacket and evaporated very quickly. He was a little damp, but the shower coming down barely made him wet.

I started to say his name, ask him a question, but he crouched behind the dumpster as we heard a car turn onto our street. I joined him. The car pulled up in front of our abandoned building and honked. A minute or so later Goldfinger came out with an umbrella in one hand and a brown paper bag in the other. Jim and I both took off running in a low crouch towards the car. He was in the lead and arrived just as the pimp got to the passenger side and the window started rolling down.
Jim was beside the driver's window in a flash. His fist sailed through the wet barrier in a hail of broken glass and a shattering sound. It was raining hard, but I could

still hear The Hammer's cry of surprise which then turned to pain as Jim dragged him out of the car through the window. I may have heard bones breaking too, I don't know. Jim slammed him on the ground, raised one fist and brought it down with a sickening crunch onto the man's face. His jaw broke and I saw some teeth fly onto the street. Jim dropped him onto the pavement where blood and drool began to mix with the rain.

I was in awe, just staring with gun in hand, at Jim as this happened. Then there was a simultaneous crack of gunfire and sound of glass breaking as the rear window of the vehicle next to me exploded. I dropped to my knee and turned around. Four men were in the alley coming up behind us. They were running towards the street while shooting through a broken, rusted chain-link fence that surrounded the empty lot between the alley and Goldfinger's whorehouse.

I brought my gun up, took a deep breath, and steadied my hands. Firing three quick shots as the men passed the remainder of the fence and started down the street towards us, my gun answered theirs. One of them went down and I heard Jim's gun going off as bullets went over my head. Jim moved up close to me and took a position a little farther into the street, away from the car, and ahead of me. He was in the open. With both of us firing back, the two thugs still on their feet backed into the alley behind the dumpster. The four of us fired shots at each other over and over. Bullets punched holes into the car I was behind and ricocheted off the brick behind our enemies.

Just as my gun emptied, I saw Goldfinger creep up between me and Jim. He had a gun in his left and a knife in his right. Thinking he was with us, I grabbed a mag and started to reload. The next thing I knew, Goldfinger brought that knife up and plunged it into Jim's back. Seeing the betrayal too late, I tried to yell.

What happened next will forever be etched into my brain. It was like slow motion watching that knife bite through Jim's coat and into flesh, but as it did, something unnatural happened. Where the knife cut Jim's skin a blue flame erupted out. The flame engulfed the knife and Goldfinger's hand. Goldfinger had leveled his gun at me, but with the fire came pain. As the heat and flame coated his hand he jumped behind us, the knife still in Jim's back. Dropping his gun, Goldfinger clutched a black, smoking thing that had been his fingers and palm. He was screaming in agony. Jim just stood up and turned around as he reached for the knife in his back. He reached up and pulled it out. I could see the thing glowed a dull red as he held it, turning black in spots where the rain struck. He rammed that hot knife into Goldfinger's heart.

While this was happening, more shots rang out from the alley. One struck Jim and I could see another momentary flash of fire and blue light where the bullet hit him in the back. Jim calmly turned around. As he did, one could see a blue light radiating from his eyes. He raised his gun and started walking towards the alley, slowly taking aim and firing. The thugs in the alley fired a fevered volley at him. Twice they hit him and both times came the flame and light pouring from his skin and eyes. Freaking out from this supernatural spectacle, they started running down the alley. And who can blame them? I was freaking out too. He shot them both in the back before there was too much distance between them and us. Reloading while he slowly walked up that alley, he cast a glance my way. The blue light was gone from his eyes. One thug lay still and the other writhed and screamed in pain. He shot the man lying there to finish him off. Then he reached down and grabbed the live one by the ankle and began dragging him back towards me.

The man screamed for mercy, but Jim just kept dragging him along the pavement until he got to the steps of the whorehouse. The man was begging by then, but Jim hoisted him up those steps and pulled him through the front door. I, dumbfounded by what had just happened, regained my wits and stuffed the remaining three bodies in the trunk of the car. Driving it a few blocks away, I then wiped my prints off the inside, and ran back. By the time I got there, the whores who made their living in the basement were upstairs looking at me in total fear. There were muffled cries below and a calm, deep voice answering. Before I got to the bottom of the stairs, I heard a bone crack and the cries stopped.

I entered the room and Jim was wiping his hands. The man's head lolled to the side, tongue partway out.

"He said Lanza authorized a hit on us, well me really, 50 grand is the price. The rest of you are collateral, but no money on your heads, yet." Jim said nodding at the dead goon.

I looked at Jim and then his jacket. The coat, a once nice blazer, he had discarded on one of the beds. There were bullet holes in it. They were in his shirt too and there were red blood stains and burnt cloth where the bullets had struck him. His skin was clean, though, showing not even a scratch. "Jim, what the fuck is going on?" I said waving at the holes in his shirt and where they should have been in his body.

"I'll tell you later, but for now, give me your jacket." He was taking off his shirt at that point and took my coat to wear. He left the ruined sports coat and shirt on the floor in the whorehouse. I grabbed the ruined things before leaving. Jim might not have cared, but it still mattered if we left evidence.

My car was hidden in an abandoned warehouse a few blocks away. We checked the street through the windows, and when we could see it was clear, quickly walked to it and headed to Oakland to meet Marty and Red.

Chapter 12

Revelation

As soon as we were on the road, I nearly yelled the same question at him, "What the fuck is going on Jim? You kicked that door in at The Wharf, and tonight I saw you get shot, SHOT! What the hell was that fire?" In my amazement and fear, I was about to start ranting, but he put his hand on my shoulder in the familiar way.

"Alright, alright, calm down. I'll tell you." He said.

We were on the Bay Bridge headed to Oakland. The rain was coming down hard again. The windshield wipers were going fast, but it wasn't enough. The lights of oncoming cars were blurry in my vision. The lamps on the side passing one after the other in a blurred, almost blinding light. The bridge was crowded with lots of cars heading out of the city. It was one of those dark rainy nights where you're concerned about what you can see because even through all the rain and glare, other cars were close, too close.

"It's the stone." He said. "It has something in it, magic maybe."

"You mean the one the old man gave you? A magic stone? Magic, Jim? Are you messed in the head or what?"

He turned towards me. I could see him out of the corner of my eye, but I couldn't look straight at him. The road was too wet, dark, and dangerous. "That old codger didn't give it to me, though he did call it good luck. He didn't heal me either, the stone did that after I found it in some old building in the jungle."

After that last bit, he went silent, thinking. Then "It whispers to me, Jake. It talks, but I don't understand it. I think it needed someone, anyone and I was the only one close. I was chosen because I was there, but I'm not sure it thinks I'm a good choice. It's power. The fire, the light, think about it. Tonight, I got shot and stabbed. You saw it all. There's not a mark on me, but I did get shot. I did get stabbed. I'm stronger now, a lot stronger, a bit faster too. But there are other effects, side effects maybe."

"Side effects?"

"I don't sleep much anymore, and I can't get drunk. Something's going on. It has a purpose. It's waking up from a long rest and refuses to sleep."

His hand was at his chest now, fingering the stone on the black leather strap around his neck. I could have sworn I saw it pulse blue briefly, but then it was just a necklace. We passed a lamp that reflected off the gray-blue hood of my car. As the light passed through the cab I could see Jim in my jacket, dry as could be. The lamp illuminated his face from the far side but there was still shadow over the profile close to me. There was a dim blue glow in his eye, visible only because of the dark. As the streetlight passed, so too did the illumination and I could see the glow a bit more distinctly, yet still faint. Or maybe it was just his blue eyes.

"Think what we can do with it Jakey. Think what we can accomplish. Lanza owns the cops, The Wharf, the streets. It won't be enough." He mused. "I'll kill them all if I have to."

That last bit filled me with momentary confidence. With Jim invincible, we could win this war that seemed to us unwinnable. But then I started to think on his last words. He'd kill them all if he had to, but so would they. They would kill us all if they could. The rest of us didn't have the power, The Stone. We had no light in our eyes, no fire under our skin, and if we got shot, that would be the end of it.

We sat in silence for the rest of the drive. I turned off the freeway shortly after crossing the bridge and drove a few blocks inland to a shitty Motel 6. Jim hopped out and got us a room. We had chosen this location because we could park in the back and our cars would not be visible from the street. While I waited, I glanced around through the blurry windows. It was a dark night and the most visible thing was the red and blue 6 sign on a post by the road. I tried to see who was in the cars passing by, but it was no use. Jim exited pretty quickly with our room keys and I pulled us around back.

I could see Marty's car as we pulled up and parked a few spaces over. I grabbed a couple of duffle bags out of the trunk and headed in with our stuff, what little we had of it. Jim went to knock on Marty's room a couple doors down. As I entered my spirit sank unconsciously. I looked around the cheap room with the worn green carpet, sick and slightly brown from use. The TV was an old-style coin-operated black and white. The beds were made, but the comforters and pillow covers were that same sick and faded green. I wondered if I was going to die there.

I had thrown a couple coins in the TV and was watching some crappy show or another when I heard a key in the door. Thinking it was Jim, I still put my hand on the butt of my gun. As the door opened, I relaxed minutely as I saw his black hair and blue eyes. Marty and Red followed him in, each holding a worn chair that the motel had in each room as an amenity. Jim looked calm as ever. The other two wore worried looks on their faces.

"It's just us," Jim smiled, glancing at my hand. Then he nodded at the table with chipped linoleum and the same sort of crappy chairs the guys were carrying. I got up and after moving the table out to give all four chairs room, set the gun down close by and took a seat. The chair I took was worse than the others. The back had partly broken away on one side and one of its roller wheels was jammed. The cramped quarters and that shitty chair seemed an appropriate reflection of our situation.

Marty had a half-full bottle of bourbon and we busted out some glasses. You know the kind, the hotel's flimsy, plastic water glasses wrapped in paper. Red raised his nearly full glass and said, "To Stitch". Thinking the worst, I looked from face to face and all three wore a sad expression. "Oh no..." I said, and Red interrupted me.

"We got a call from The Old Man, they ran into some trouble. Stark got away, but he said they managed to catch Stitch. Apparently, he got shot in the gut and couldn't run anymore. Stark is on his way here now, but he's taking the scenic route in case he's being followed."

We raised our glasses and in unison "To Stitch."

A few hours and an empty bottle of bourbon later, The Old Man found his way to us. He had switched cabs more than once, taken a bus or two, and after being satisfied he wasn't followed, walked the last few blocks in the rain. He knocked on our door to let us know he arrived, took his room key from Jim, and went and sacked out.

If Lanza knew where we were, we would have known it by then. He would have sent some guys after us. That meant that Stitch had not snitched for some reason. He was most likely dead. We took turns keeping watch that night, one of us always awake keeping an eye on the parking lot. The rest of us slept troubled sleep when it wasn't our turn.

Chapter 13

Another War, Another Army

I dreamed again that night.

I stood on the beach again. It was as if I had never moved. The shore stretched from horizon to horizon, left to right, in a great crescent. The sand glittered white and tan and silver under the combined lights of sun, moon, and stars.

The all-encompassing trumpets began to sound, and I looked to the man who was not Jim striding across the water towards the darkness. The black cloud had grown, devouring more sea, sky, and beach. Light and fire still poured from him, and as the trumpets devoured all other sound, new figures began to take shape around him. A bird with wings of storm glided down from the sky and transformed into a man, brown-skinned and nearly naked save for leather around his waist. He landed abreast of Jim and also walked towards the darkness. A column of ice rose from the water leaving an ashen colored man in gray wolf skins holding a spear. He also walked toward the darkness. A tan-skinned woman with golden hair formed out of sunlight next to Jim and walked. She wore nothing but a gold skirt. A wave of water rose and transformed into a black-haired woman. She wore silk robes adorned in cherry blossoms. She too walked beside the others. A spectral form made of stars coalesced into a ghostly image of a woman. She too walked. And finally, a woman born from the space between the stars, cloaked in falcon feathers and carrying a golden scepter. She alighted upon the water and she too walked with the others towards the darkness.

The seven figures marched on, walking across The Ocean. Their footsteps landing in unison, their stride equal and abreast. They raised their hands, almost as if one, and the powers of creation lanced forward towards the bottomless, black cloud devouring the world. Fire and lightning and ice and waves and rays of sunlight and starlight and death and All streaked forward. The abyss recoiled from the assault, pulling back, leaving nothing but formless gray where it had been. Then the abyss, turbulent and angry, lashed out. I saw columns of inky nothingness stretch towards the figures.

I awoke with a start. A terror of the void had gripped me and then subsided.

Jim sat in one of the shitty chairs by the window. He seemed to not have noticed me stirring. His chin rested on his hand as he stared out at the grimy parking lot. A brown paper trash bag blew across the parking spaces getting caught in a puddle and quickly sticking to the pavement. His bed was still made, and I slipped back into a troubled slumber.

Chapter 14

Jim Heads Out

When I woke up later in the morning, Jim was gone. He had taken my car. The other three men were up and coming back from breakfast. They were surprised to see me having assumed that I went with him. The car had been gone when they woke up.

We were all worried, although, in truth, I was not as concerned as I might have been in different circumstances. Whatever Jim was doing, he had The Stone and its mysterious power. No one else had seen it. We had not spoken about his abilities or his strength except the previous night in the car. In fact, while recounting to the boys what had happened with Goldfinger, Jim left some parts out. No one else had seen his power and while discussing the fight, he didn't mention it or that he had been hurt. It was not something for me to volunteer so I remained quiet. I didn't know the extent the power had changed him, but I knew he would likely be OK. His bullet and stab wounds had healed almost immediately after all.

I headed over to the breakfast joint to fill my own belly. The restaurant was one of those run-down places you see standing alone on a city corner. Surrounded by dirty parking lots and next to an old rusted train track, it was a testament to failed ambition. Years ago, someone had put a lot of money into the art deco building with a huge sign above it. It spoke to everyone who passed it by on the freeway or one of Oakland's main streets. Or at least it tried to. Now the round metal pylons that held it up were streaking rust

64

from spots coming through all the white paint. The sign itself was faded and sun-bleached. The building, once white and blue, was dirty and also faded. Oil stains and trash marred the lots around the structure. A few beat up and rusting cars gave an indication of the people within. A dent here and broken window there, all were evidence of the lack of money or care the people within possessed.

The hostess seated me, and I ordered a simple breakfast of eggs, bacon, and pancakes. The food was the cheap, low flavor stuff found in similar establishments throughout poorer towns. The syrup was the thick sugar water with color added to make it appear like the real thing.

Alone, I had time to ponder my dream and what Jim had said to me the night before "...but I'm not sure it thinks I'm a good choice." The words echoed in my head. The Stone, the power in it, the dreams of a man with ancient eyes that had to be related to it. Lost in my thoughts deep enough I could easily have been a target. I didn't even notice my food had been delivered to the table. Maybe twenty minutes into my reverie, I realized someone could easily have taken me out. Putting the thoughts out of my head I endeavored to eat the cooling breakfast while keeping my eyes open.

On the walk back to the vomit green motel room, I saw Jim pull into the parking lot. He was moving slowly as he got out of the car, retrieving a duffle from the trunk. I was surprised to see him looking worn out and a bit tired. His hair was matted on one side and stuck to his head. I could see dried blood there, and my borrowed jacket covered more blood still on his shirt. He waved a tired hand at me as I approached, lurched towards the motel room door and went in. I followed.

I let the door close behind me. He was already stripping down. His torn shirt was off, and I could see blood dried all over his skin. "Don't worry," he said, "it's not all mine." With that, he stumbled into the white tile bathroom, started the shower and slipped into the stall. He came out a few minutes later all cleaned up and motioned his hand at my questioning face "Let me sleep first." With that he was out, snoring softly almost as soon as he hit one of the twin beds that filled the tiny room. I took the bloody clothes and drove a ways away to dump them in a crappier part of the crappy town. Sitting for a couple weeks in a nearly full dumpster will bury a lot of evidence.

When he woke, he told me the story. After learning that Stitch was likely dead, he decided to get some payback. Realizing he had an advantage the rest of us did not share, he went after Crispy without us.

He had left just before first light. Jim knew that Crispy had some early morning business to deal with down at the Pacific Crab Company on The Wharf. It was a regular thing for the crew down there. It was also where our shipment was supposed to come in.

Jim had parked my Buick a few blocks away and cautiously made his way to the pier. The building was set back about 50 feet from the boat dock that a lot of the companies there shared. It was a two-story, warehouse-like building with a few windows and a truck dock on the land side. On the ocean side were cutting stations and boards where crabs and fish could be processed. A slide existed so that the refuse from the day's catch could be washed back into the ocean for scavengers to eat or simply to rot. On the land side was a large, white sign with red stenciled words of the company name and contact information. There was a big rolling door at the truck dock to load processed meat onto a hauler. To the left side was the front of the building and featured some windows and signs welcoming customers. To the right was the back door and a single window on the second story. Light spilled from that window into the early morning twilight. Jim could hear raucous yelling from the room as the men inside enjoyed whatever they were doing.

Jim went to the front door. He thought that it was farthest from the men on the second story and they would be less likely to hear. Moving up to the glass door framed in aluminum, he pushed until the lock or frame broke. He entered and quickly passed through the small walled office area. It was a typical office, set up with generic walls, desks, and chairs, looking almost temporary as warehouse offices often do. The sound of the front door breaking brought the lone guard into the cubicles from inside the warehouse. It was Ricky DeLano, Bull's younger brother. Think of Bull but a little younger and a little smaller, in case you haven't seen the pictures. Jim closed the distance between them quickly. Ricky drew his revolver and fired hitting Jim in the gut, but of course, there was only a flash of light and fire and then Jim was on him. He snapped Ricky's neck in less than a heartbeat.

Jim picked up Ricky's gun and barreled through the office door into the warehouse. It was a wide-open space with processing equipment and then conveyor belts that led to packaging machines. There was also a staircase midway through the space leading up to the offices on the second floor. Hearing the shots, a couple of bruisers were rushing down the stairs to confront our leader. By this point, he had Ricky's gun in one hand and his military-style .45 in the other. A gunfight ensued with him blazing both guns while the two muscles fired back. He killed them both as he emptied his own two weapons. But he was hit at least three times he told me. Of course, when he was shot, there was the burst of blue fire, but something happened and when he told me about it, I started to worry. The wounds did not heal immediately. He could feel the pain and when he looked at his stomach where the bullets had hit, he could see blue ichor pulsing and struggling to fix him.

He discarded Ricky's revolver, reloaded his .45, and headed up the stairs. Another bout of shooting happened as he pushed his way up the steps. Crispy and the rest of his guys were waiting for Jim. He killed a couple, shooting until his gun was empty. Then he took a few more shots as he moved around the room tearing flesh, breaking bones, and crushing skulls with his empty pistol and supernatural strength. It was one of those shots that grazed his head, causing the blood that had matted his hair. In the mayhem, Crispy jumped through the window, getting caught on broken glass as he fled. Jim finished off the rest of the men, moving around the room, around the remnants of the poker game on the table, killing whoever was standing. He took shot after shot, felt pain after pain, as the power he possessed became less and less effective. When all were dead he rushed to the window, dripping blue ichor that turned to crimson blood as it fell from his body. He could see Crispy hurriedly limping away, a leg damaged from the fall or perhaps one of Jim's bullets.

His own gun empty, he grabbed a pistol off the floor and shot through the window trying to finish the fleeing man.

He missed.

Hearing sirens in the distance and almost faint with pain, Jim made his own retreat. By the time he got to my car, his wounds had healed, but he confided in me that he had left a lot of blood on sidewalks as he rushed to the vehicle. He was also certain that Crispy had seen the power, the blue fire and the light, as Jim got shot. With wide eyes and a shocked expression, he had seen Jim move with inhuman force through the room, slaughtering The Wharf goons. And of course, Crispy was still alive to talk.

When our other boys were notified, Jim told them a version of the story that was almost as incredible as if he had described his powers. He left that part out, of course, but our guys were wondering how he could have taken on so many bruisers and not gotten shot or killed. You could tell that they were almost disbelieving but that also hope had lit a fire within them. The dark malaise of worry and sadness that had settled over them from losing Stitch, that seemed to permeate the motel and even Oakland itself, was somehow burning away.

Chapter 15
The Loss Confirmed

The phone rang. Stark and I were at the table sharing another bottle of bourbon while Jim dozed on the bed. The ringing stirred him from his sleep, but I was already answering the line.

"Your boy is at Molloy's". My blood froze as I heard Crispy speak those words. They knew where we were. He knew what motel to call and in what town. That meant Stitch had talked. I pulled the curtain back and looked outside. "You hear me?" Crispy followed up when I didn't answer. No one was outside that I could see.

"Yeah, I heard you, you wop, traitor motherfucker." The words spilled from my mouth without thought. Stark and Jim stood up, grabbing their iron. Both checked the window, pistols in hand, while Crispy continued. "The Boss says you can put your man to rest. He was a good man, loyal to the end. Lanza says you can have a couple of days, then we'll finish it."

"That's right Crispy, we'll finish it. Whatever else happens I'm going to put one in your head, you hear me you sack of shit?" They knew where we were, and I had no reason to be polite.

Crispy's voice was cautious. "We'll see." He was pensive, afraid but not wanting to show it. He had seen Jim in action and knew the threat was real despite the odds. "The Boss is pissed. You have nowhere you can run. We'll find you. Stitch went the distance, though, and because of that, he earned a good Catholic burial. Make it happen or when we catch you Stitch's last hours will look like a day at the zoo."

With that, he hung up. Stark had already left the room and I could hear him banging on Marty and Red's door. Jim was stuffing what little he had into his bags. The duffle taken from Crispy was filled with some bloody money, not much, but enough that he couldn't leave it after his battle in the warehouse. He threw a couple of guns in the bag, some shirts and other things and after I finished doing the same, we headed out the door.

We went across the bay to the projects in Sausalito. The town was in a nice area as landscape went, a few miles from the beach and spotted with the pines and other serene characteristics that made Marin County what it was. The projects themselves were ugly, multistory buildings supposed to make life easier for people without money. In reality, they became cesspools of drug use and gang life set back from the better part of town between two foothills. There were multiple buildings and, in another life, another world maybe, they could have been luxury apartments. This was our world, though, and whatever good intentions those structures started with, they had been taken over by lowlifes. I know, I know, our crew probably fits your definition of lowlife. Maybe poor, stupid, and desperate would have been a better description.

We made our way to the fifth floor where Red had a woman. When she opened the door, it was clear she wasn't too happy to see him. She tried to hide her fear as the five of us moved inside her rundown, two-bedroom apartment. Her name was Maria Lopez, and I could see why Red had taken a fancy to her. She was dark-haired, voluptuous and beautiful with that hint of defiance in her eyes that attracted most men.

Maria and Red started talking and it quickly became a heated exchange. Maria was afraid, her eyes would smolder a smoky allure under normal circumstances, but this day they were wide with fear. As the talk turned to raised voices to shouting, I looked past Maria deeper into the apartment. A small girl stared at the two from the floor between a couch and coffee table. She had some dolls on that table, but they were forgotten as tears welled up in her eyes and she started to silently cry. I heard a crack and jerked my head back to see the tail end of the slap Red hand landed on Maria.

"HEY!!" I yelled and grabbed Red pushing him up against the wall. "We're not doing it this way." Maria was holding her face a red mark where the slap had hit her. The rest of the boys, even Jim, were silent. I couldn't tell if it was from the sound of the slap or my yelling.

"You", I pointed at Maria, "take your girl into a bedroom. I promise we won't hurt her or you again. We'll talk in a little bit."

"YOU!!" I put my finger in Red's face, "sit your ass on that couch and cool off, have a beer or whatever, but if you touch her again, I'll fuck you up."

Red was both surprised and angry, but when he glanced at Jim he got an almost imperceptible nod and did what he was told. I could see on Jim's face a slight smile, something akin to pride. I look back on that situation now with my own pride, but at the time I was just pissed. To be honest, I don't know what came over me. We were all out of sorts, all stressed out and upset over Stitch. I was pretty sure we were going to die, except maybe Jim, and I guess I really didn't want one of my last memories to be like when we grew up.

Maria moved quickly to the living room shooing the girl, Alma, and gathering the dolls. The rest of us finished entering the apartment and closed the door as the mother took her daughter through the kitchen and into a smaller room next to it. After a few words telling the young girl that it would be alright she closed the door and turned to face us. Fear and no small amount of anger were evident on her face.

"How long are you going to be here?" She asked, trying to be calm but the anger came through anyway. She was looking at me as if I was in charge.

I looked to Jim and he was fishing through one of the bags he brought with him. Red was on the couch, a beat-up brown thing with billowy pillows, comfortable but stained from too many spilled plates or glasses. Marty had settled in next to him, it was a small couch, a love seat really. Jim sat down in a matching easy chair, just as comfortable and just as worn. Stark, the hulking man he was and with no other seats in the room, had sat on the floor opposite the couch with the hallway to the front door behind him.

"Not long we hope," I said. In reality, I was actually embarrassed to be there. It didn't seem right. Jim grunted and I could see he had laid a stack of cash on the table. I picked it up, ten $100 dollar bills free of blood.

"$500 for letting us stay here," I handed her five of the bills, then handing her the other five "$500 for your silence. We'll be safer and you'll be safer if no one knows we're here." Then I looked at Jim, then to Red, then back to Jim "Another $1000 for the slap. We're sorry." Jim looked at me for a second, then thought better of questioning me. I'd like to think we were on the same page, but I guess it's possible he just didn't want to argue. He pulled out the other ten bills and gave them to her.

Maria took the money then went to the bedroom with her daughter in it and closed the door behind her. That was a lot of money for a single mom in the projects. Also, she was from a tough neighborhood and probably knew the score. She had no idea who was after us but knew they were dangerous. If they went at us in her apartment, neither she nor the girl would be safe. It was very likely she would keep her mouth shut.

All of a sudden there was the loud buzzing of a snore coming from the floor. Stark had fallen asleep and was sounding like a god damn chainsaw. He had the old man sound, you know, the loud noise followed by a series of coughing or choking noises, then back to the snore. We all started to chuckle. Jim looked at Stark thoughtfully then leaned back and closed his eyes in the big easy chair. Red and Marty went to the kitchen table, Red not looking at me, and started playing cards. I settled in on the love seat and dozed off myself.

Powers Advance

I woke up at least an hour later, maybe more. Red and Marty were still playing cards. They each had a mug of coffee. Maria was in the kitchen fixing some food for herself and daughter. She had put a plate of baloney sandwiches on the counter for the rest of us. Judging by the crumbs on the table and a hint of mayonnaise at the corner of Marty's mouth, he had already eaten.

It could have been the noise, but what I really think woke me up was this sensation in my head. I had been dreaming, but about what I couldn't tell you, just that in the dream I had felt a tug, something in my mind, and when I woke up that feeling persisted. Looking around that small apartment, it was easy to see that Jim was gone.

"Where's Jim?" I asked.

"He went out, didn't say where. He's been gone a couple of hours." Maria had answered me when Red didn't, and Marty was in mid swig of coffee. She nodded her chin at the plate of sandwiches, "Help yourself." She made eye contact with me and held it for a second, then went back to cooking. I was glad to see there was no mark still on her face.

A couple of hours she had said. Time must have advanced faster than I thought, or my sleep lasted longer. Clearly, we needed the rest. Red still wouldn't look at me, but his shoulders drooped as if he was tired. Marty was fading. Stark was still snoring that buzz saw sound on the floor. I had only come awake because of the mental sensation.

The tugging feeling kept up, getting stronger, like an urgent curiosity. I hopped up, grabbed a baloney sandwich and let the feeling take me. I headed out the door and into the dirty corridor of the building. Wandering to the tune of the strange feeling, I found myself at an emergency stairwell and started heading up. For some reason, it was up that I had to go. The stairs were dark, the cheap lighting long since broken out. Looking upwards toward the door, with light streaming in around the edges, reminded one of moving through a dark tunnel and seeing the sunlight at the end. Upon reaching the top, I finished the rest of my sandwich and pushed open the door that had long since lost its lock. A view of the top of the building with the peaks of the foothills beyond greeted me. Empty beer cans, broken needles, and other refuse littered the asphalt and pebble roof. At the edge I could see Jim standing, leaning on one leg, looking over the side of the building.

"It can do other things Jakey," Jim said without turning around. He knew my footsteps or otherwise had sensed my approach. His face was angled downwards as if looking at what was below, but his eyes were closed. My gaze followed his, or where he would have been looking had his eyes been open. They were closed when I reached him. A short distance from the building there was a grove of weeping willows that grew where the two foothills met. The grove stretched up the valley as it ascended where the mountains grew together.

"There is a wind coming. It will hit the trees right... now." He pointed towards the highest point of the grove as he said the last word. The willow branches began rustling down the direction of the slope. It was like a wave hitting the trees and washing all the way to the parking lot they grew next to. He turned to me as he opened his eyes and looked at what had to be the dubious expression on my face.

"Look." He bent over and picked up a piece of cardboard lying on the roof next to us. He tore a small piece off and held it in the palm of his hand as the breeze below reached us. He concentrated on that bit of paper and the wind caught it. It traveled up, carried by the air, and impossibly arced back against the wind and finally settled again into his palm after completing a circle. There was a look of stress and beads of sweat on his face. The little show had taken some effort.

"That's great Jim, very interesting, but I'm worried about this power of yours." Pushing past my amazement at his spectacle and focusing on the worries that had been gnawing at me. "You're not healing as fast as you were. You left blood all over The Wharf. What's going on? Is the power running out?"

"I don't know. I don't think so, but maybe."

"Is it like a battery that runs out? You're getting tired when you use it. I can see it on your face, and you slept." I pressed.

"It could be, but yeah, I don't think so. I told you, it thinks I'm a bad choice. It's holding back. It still needs me, so it's there, but not as willing."

"Willing? What is this thing?" My question hung there for a few seconds.

"I think it's a god, Jakey, an ancient god. I get the feeling it was waking up from a long sleep or something when I found it. It showed me things, in my mind and dreams. I saw it, or me, or us walking across a great ocean and warring with some other, darker power." When he said this, my blood froze. "There are others too. They're out there. I can feel them." That chilled me even more.

"Willing, though, Jim? Will it be there when we need it?" I continued focusing on my initial worries.

He paused for a bit, then with that ever-confident gaze "It will be there. Come on, let's go get Stitch."

We had started walking towards the open door that led down the stairs and into the project. The thoughts about what he had said tumbled through my mind. An ancient god walking on the ocean and doing battle. Had the thing been in my head? Was it talking to me too?

Chapter 17

Stitch

Aidan "Stitch" Campbell was a San Francisco native. Like a lot of the guys in our line of work, he had it rough growing up. Unlike a lot of us, in his younger days, it looked like he was going to come out of our neighborhood OK. He worked the odd job, even while he was in the life, and generally kept his head down. Putting himself through City College, he earned an Associate's degree and went on to nursing school. He landed a nice job at a local hospital and basically had it made, on paper at least. In reality, he never left the life. For a few years, he was living like the upper class, making good money in the medical field, making more selling painkillers and other things he stole from his day job. Eventually, he was caught, arrested, and sentenced to just under two years in jail for his activities. It would have been more, but they couldn't connect him with a lot of the theft as he'd been smart about it. Plus, he kept his mouth shut. He lost his nursing license.

Now, a lot of the guys used to give him shit because he was a male nurse. That all stopped when they realized he was the one they would go to to get stitched up if they got beaten badly, stabbed, or shot. It was easy to want to razz him too. He was a thinner guy, his brownish-reddish hair thinning on top, and with ashen, pale skin he looked older than he was. The wire-rimmed glasses didn't help either. The insults usually stopped when a person realized they needed him to dig a bullet out, or he punched you in the nose.

He didn't look like much, and he certainly wasn't like Stark, but he was like the rest of us. That meant if he swung, you got hurt. Anyway, he was one of the "go-to" guys in the city if you needed some cut sewed up or something.

The San Francisco underbelly lost a good man. We confirmed it when we opened the trunk of Stitch's car behind Molloy's. He had already started to smell, but just barely. By the looks of him, his last few hours had been his worst. I won't go into much detail here, and you won't see any reports on it either, but to give you an idea, most of his face wasn't recognizable and he was missing some fingers. I guess Crispy wasn't kidding about him being loyal. Either that or they just wanted some revenge.

"Motherfucker!" Red said loudly, almost at a yell. All of us were in shock when the trunk was opened and we saw what Lanza's boys had left of our friend. Red started ranting, "Those motherfuckers, those god damn wops, those..." and he continued ranting. Marty joined in with him, talking about how they were going to kill everyone. Stark took off his jacket and laid it over Stitch's torso and head. His own face was a seething mask of rage, but he wasn't speaking. I looked at Jim from the side. He wore a grim look, one of controlled anger, but just barely controlled. I saw his fists clench. I heard thunder in the distance, or maybe it was just the trunk shutting. He looked at me, though, and for a moment, the blue light grew faintly in his eyes. It was broad daylight, any of the boys could have seen it, but as I near as I could tell none of them did.

We checked Stitch's car for bombs, car bombs really were a gangland thing back then. Satisfied it was clean, Jim and Stark jumped in to take Stitch for burial. The car was beat to crap, but not from anything the Mob's men had done. Stitch, even though he had had decent money, just liked driving the thing. He was always talking about putting cash into it. You couldn't tell by the look of it. The car was a late 60's Chevelle with sun-beaten dark green paint and a lime green racing stripe from front to back on the right side. The panels had dings and one of the rims was just rust. You could hear the money when Jim started it up, though. It was a big engine and it purred like a lion. When Jim pulled out, I followed. Marty and Red went back inside Molloy's for a little business and told us they would meet us later.

We headed to Donagan's Mortuary. Now Donagan's was an Irish Catholic business. It was in a more rundown part of town and boasted good prices. It was, of course, one of those dumpy mortuaries that prey on the recently grieving. Their initial services were cheap enough to be inviting, but the average person will soon be met by a salesperson who comes complete in a polyester suit and with greased back hair. It's that grease jobs role to up-sell the broken families to high-end coffins or elaborate urns. He will bring brochures with pictures of ornate resting boxes that are lined with expensive fabrics and say things like "I'm just here to help you help your family". He would coax children into paying outlandish prices for coffins to cremate their parents in. The racket is designed to play upon the lapse in judgment caused by a death in the family. More than one family paid for a coffin that never made it to the crematorium. Bodies would be removed from the nice coffins in the back room so the box itself could be resold. The body would be burned in a cheaper vessel. I can just imagine the families walking down the hallways filled with worn, marble plaques visiting the ashes of their loved ones or passing through to the graveyard behind. They would be none the wiser that in their moments of pain, they were being stolen from just a couple of rooms over. It's probably better for them to never know.

It's only now, years later, that I realize how disgusting that place really was.

Donagan's was also a place in our network. Back then, due to the sanctity of a coffin, things could be smuggled in and out of the country in one. Sometimes even people if the price was right. Stitch had also spent some time there. Because of the equipment for preparing bodies for burial, it was an ideal place he could perform medical procedures on the wayward criminal in need of help. It didn't happen too often with members of The Family close or distant, because like I said, Lanza kept The Family small. But smaller hoods and thugs would visit that place on a regular basis. So, that's where we went. They even had a Priest on call who could come when needed. That's what we wanted, a proper Catholic burial for our friend.

Joe Donagan was not too happy to see us. He was less happy when he saw what happened to Stitch. He agreed to take care of our friend for us, and in a timely manner. Stitch's body was moved to the

backroom and the morticians went to work. Joe called
the Priest. Even so, the process took a few hours.
During that time, a few of our new recruits showed up,
the ones from the restaurant and bag job. At least one
of them had been patched up by Stitch on a prior
occasion. The others were probably there because they
knew an opening had occurred in our group and
wanted to show loyalty. I doubted any of them would
have come if they knew the full extent of the trouble
we were in.

We all waited, using the time to chat and
reflect on Stitch. We also talked about what we were
going to do when we were done. I don't know how
long after, but we had been there a while when a limo
with three other cars pulled up. A number of Lanza's
thugs, ten maybe fifteen, started exiting the vehicles.
One entered the building. At this point, we had all
migrated to the service room and were waiting for
Stitch in his coffin to be brought out. Our new recruits
were starting to get nervous. All except the one Stitch
had stitched up. His name was Sean and I noticed he
just had a grim, stoic look on his face. A lone thug
entered the mortuary and found us in the service room,
hands behind our backs or in our coats. We all were
alert with a hand on our iron. He scanned the room and
his eyes settled on Jim.

"Mr. Jones, The Boss would like a chat." He
said.

"Fuck that." Red spat, getting a hard stare from
the thug.

"He's here to pay his respects. Nothing will happen unless you start it." The thug had switched his gaze back to Jim while he talked.

Jim looked around the room at us and paused briefly on me. Then he looked back at Lanza's man and nodded to him while heading out the door.

"Get ready, I don't know if we can trust these guys," I said as they went outside. I could do Jim's calculation in my head. With his power he was safe, but he was worried about us. More than one assassination had happened at a criminal's funeral. The math in my head was the same, but that's only if the power held. If it didn't, he could die out in the parking lot and we would be a man down even before they came at us.

Pulling the window curtain to the side we could see Jim approach the limo. As he did, one of the thugs opened the rear door and Lanza himself stepped out. He was using a cane and he was an old bastard, even then, but I can tell you he didn't need it. He had it for show. Whatever else he was, Lanza was a tough son of a bitch, even in his old age. Jim and Lanza began talking, with Jim keeping his hands respectfully clasped in front of him. Lanza seemed cordial enough, but he did motion here or there. We couldn't hear what he was saying but Jim told me later that Crispy and his guys were on the far side of the graveyard. At least that's what Lanza said, which, turned out to be true. At one point during the exchange, Jim turned his head and looked towards the window. He could have killed Lanza then and there but with the number of guys surrounding Donagan's he didn't think we would make it, even if he did. Sometimes I wish he had done it anyway. San Francisco probably would have been better off without the likes of Lanza and us, if I'm being honest. In the end, I guess it didn't matter much.

Jim and Lanza turned towards the mortuary and walked in together, flanked by Lanza's guys. When they arrived the two of them took a position in the front row. I sat behind them and one of Lanza's torpedoes sat next to me, eyeing my hand resting on my lap near the butt of my gun.

"Take it easy Jake, The Boss is just here to pay respect to Stitch." It was Victor "Vic" Flinn. He had been one of our guys before Jim disappeared. He had joined Mustache's crew. The tension was evident in his face and posture. Maybe it was because he knew us, probably because of the situation. Most likely it was both.

I nodded. "Good to see you, Vic. Just the same, you reach for your piece and it's over for you."

"Now boys, be nice. We're just chatting here. Keep it civil." Lanza said as he turned his head to address us. He was polite but his voice held the firmness of command.

A side door to the service room opened. Joe Donagan was there and when he saw Lanza, his face went pale and he stopped. The Boss nodded at Joe and waved his hand in a motion for him to continue. Donagan and another mortician wheeled Stitch's coffin out, followed by the Priest. They left the lid down. I guess they couldn't repair Stitch enough for a final viewing. I considered putting one in the back of

Lanza's head then but knew if I did Flinn would put me down next.

The Priest began the service and Lanza started talking in a fairly quiet voice. "Jimmy my boy, you know I always liked you. Why didn't you run?"

"Run, Boss? I don't think so. Crispy and you can't have what's ours." Jim said in an equally quiet tone.

"Everything in this city is mine, Jimmy, you know that. Had you run, my reach would have stopped at the bridge. Now because of what you've done, the restaurant, The Wharf, killing so many of our guys, we'll find you wherever you go." He brushed back a wisp of his white hair.

"Shouldn't be too hard. We're here until it's finished. How do you know what's yours won't be mine when we're done?" Jim replied a little louder. I could see his shoulders tensing.

A feral look crossed Lanza's face. The old man was a badass and knew it. I could see the almost eager grin in his eyes when faced with a challenge, one he expected to win, but a challenge none the less. "You're going to die Jim. That much is certain, whether it's in this city or some third world shit hole you hide in, doesn't make a difference." Then he waved his hand around the room, "But what about Jake and the boys? If you run, I'll go easy on them. I'll make sure they have work. I will take care of them."

"Like you did while I was gone?" Jim replied. "Like you did when I got back? You fucked us, old man."

Lanza sighed and stood up. The Priest stopped his sermon. "Have it your way Jimmy. What happens to them is on you. Finish giving Stitch his rest. You're safe here until the service is over. After that, well, that's between you and Alberto. When he's done, I'll give you the same respect I gave Stitch."

"See you soon, Boss," Jim said after he too had stood up. Lanza gave a little nod, almost bored and walked out. His men went with him. Soon the parking lot was empty except for our cars.

We finished laying Stitch to rest. The ceremony ended with us in the graveyard throwing dirt onto a coffin after it had been lowered into the final resting spot. At the far side of the graves, through the chain-link fence stood Crispy and a bunch of his guys. We were outnumbered but stared them down anyway. They turned and headed to their cars. We did the same.

Chapter 18

The Chase

Three of the recruits had their own car. Marty and Red were still a team. Stark got into Stitch's car. As we were passing it, we could smell the bleach Donagan's guys had used to clean the trunk. That's another service Donagan's performed on the sly, clean up.

Jim and I got in my Buick. Sean joined us. "I'm with you guys from here on out," Sean said as he opened the door and sat in my backseat uninvited. "I had an idea what was going on when we started the other jobs. I don't think the other guys did, but they sure know now."

"If they're smart, if you're smart, you'll run," I said without turning my head. That got a sharp look from Jim.

"I don't know about the other guys, but for me, not a chance. Stitch took care of me a couple years back, good care of me. I want a piece of the dudes who did this." He replied. I could see a look of determination on his face in the rear-view mirror.

"It's your funeral." I started the car.

Jim frowned and then turned around. "Thanks for the loyalty, Sean." Then to me, "Wait for our boys to go, we go last." Then he clenched his fists, his eyes went vacant, and I could see him start to sweat. The wind picked up. "Head up the hill." Then he hung his head out the window and yelled at our boys to do the same.

Marty and Red took off like a shot followed closely by Stark and the car with the recruits. We were right behind them.

The shooting started as soon as Marty's car left the parking lot. Crispy's guys were just turning the corner when we exited and had not had enough time to set an ambush. Even still, a couple of them were hanging out windows firing at us as we went. Unfortunately for us, they were coming down the hill, the direction Jim had told us to go. Stark went straight, ignoring Jim's commands. I watched Stitch's green Chevelle move away as I turned left, following our other two cars directly towards our enemies. Then he was beyond the intervening buildings.

Sean and I drew our pistols. I hung my hand out the window shooting as I sped up the hill. Sean hung himself out shooting as well. Jim just sat there clenching his fists and concentrating. He yelled "Up the hill!! Go Go Go!"

As we sped past, there were simultaneous hails of bullets. They had more guys and I saw windows bust out of the cars ahead of me. Wildly emptying my pistol, I pushed the gas and then it was our turn. I heard the pings as lead struck my car. There was a hot flash in my leg and then pain burned itself into my head. I was hit. For a few seconds, it was absolute chaos as glass broke and holes appeared in cars on both sides of the street. Then we were past and charging up the slope.

The cars behind us whipped around in pursuit. The new recruits hung a right and sped off to the side.

It was just our two cars now, Marty's and mine and we barreled up the hill with Crispy's guys behind. As we crested the hill, Marty's car disappeared into an unbelievably dense fog that had materialized in front of us. A second later we were in it as well. I could barely see 10 feet.

"Just a little farther, then stop the car," Jim said in a calm voice. I went about another 100 yards and slammed on the brakes. "This will do. Out of the car now!" He said drawing his own pistol. The three of us piled out and Sean and I followed Jim to the side, where he crouched behind a parked car. I was limping but could see that the bullet had only grazed me. There was a hole in the seat I had been sitting on. Luckily for me, it had been traveling down and passed through a small section of my thigh before sinking into the cushion below. But damn, there was a lot of blood.

I could hear the revving engines of our pursuers as they sped down the hill towards us in the mist. The fog was too thick, and they saw my car too late. They didn't even have time to hit the brakes and just smashed right into the back of the Buick. As they did, the second car following us plowed into the first. More glass shattered and there was a sound of tearing metal as the three cars skidded and coasted to a stop partway down the hill.

"Now!" Jim yelled and started running towards the cars. I followed, limping, but along the sidewalk keeping parked cars between me and the wreckage on the street. Sean followed me. Jim charged into the mist, and as we approached all I could see was his form with a faint outline of the cars behind him. Jim had stopped running and was walking up to the wreckage of the lead car. The mist was suddenly lit with flashes of brightness as Jim emptied his gun into that vehicle. Someone inside was returning fire. Sean and I opened up on what was left of the second car. We aimed in the direction of the windows and seats where we thought Crispy's guys were. Someone tried to shoot back, and I heard a window break, but it was over in seconds.

Then in the mist, there was a flash of blue light and what was left of my car burst into flames. Jim walked towards us and as he approached, the smashed-up car still connected to mine also caught fire. Someone was still alive in it and we heard screaming. Jim just nodded at us and we followed him walking away.

A few blocks over a car could be heard pulling closer. In our heightened sense of tension, we were reaching for our guns again, but it turned out to be Stitch's car. Stark hung his head out and winked at us. The car was even more scraped up, from whatever Stark had done, but still drivable. We piled in and he took off.

We headed out of the city back to Maria's. All of us were quiet for a bit. Then Stark said "Crispy was chasing our other guys. I ran him into a parked car and flipped him the bird as we got away." He chuckled at that. Jim did too. I was in too much pain at the time, tying a dirty shirt around my wound. I did laugh later, though.

Chapter 19

A Lull

Back at Maria's, Red and Marty were playing cards again. Stark was sitting on the couch drinking a beer and watching the news. Sean was standing behind Red, back to the table, looking out the windows into the project parking lot. Jim headed up to the roof, to practice whatever it was he was learning to do. I couldn't explain it then, but at the time I felt it whenever he called upon that power, that force, to do something. It would be like a pressure or tingling in my head. Sometimes I could feel heat on the palms of my hands. Sometimes I felt Jim's fatigue at the effort.

Sean had gotten in touch with the other three guys after Stark had helped them getaway. Two of them basically said they didn't realize what we had gotten in to and were leaving town. The last guy, a dude named Louis, Lou for short, said he was with us. After a bit, Sean borrowed the keys to Stitch's car and left to pick Lou up.

Maria stuck her head out of the bedroom. I was sitting in a chair at the table, trying to re-bandage my wound. She called my name and jerked her head to tell me to come in. She took me into the bathroom and had already laid out some bandages, tape, and antibiotic cream.

"Get your pants off and sit on the toilet." She said motioning with her chin towards the worn porcelain bowl. The lid was down, and I sat and gingerly pulled my pants off, wincing at the pain it caused in the wound. "I'm going to fix this for you. I don't want you bleeding all over my apartment," she finished.

After I did what I was told, she began applying liberal amounts of the antibiotic and then bandaging my leg. It was only a flesh wound, but it was pretty big and hurt bad. I had been lucky. She basically filled it with the stuff, then tightly wrapped gauze around it. As she worked, even in my pain, I couldn't help but notice again how beautiful she was. She kept her head down mostly, not making eye contact, but when she was done, she looked up at me from her crouch in front of my leg. She had to have known what I was thinking from where I was looking, but even if she did, it appeared like she didn't notice.

Looking at me with those dark, smoky eyes she spoke, "You know, if you guys are found here, you've killed me and my daughter." Her tone was bland and neutral, but her words were cold, hard truth. She was facing it, even though she had no control over the situation, and wanted us to face it too. "You realize that right? You might already have fucking killed us. The wrong guys could be on their way here right now." An edge had crept into her voice and increased as she said her peace.

"You're right." I sighed inwardly. This lady didn't deserve the danger we put her in. Why was she in it? Because she had boned one of our guys a few months back. She didn't deserve a death sentence over that. "I'll do what I can to get us out of here. Again, I'm sorry."

She nodded and got up. Wanting out of the situation and thinking maybe I was the one to fix it for her, she had fixed my gunshot as a pretense to talk to me. I couldn't look at her after that. I mean think about it, we had put her and her innocent daughter in danger, Red had smacked her, and I was checking her out. I knew I was a fuckhead then. I know it now even years later. Luckily, as far as I heard, nothing ever happened to her. I hope she's okay.

She opened the door a minute or so after leaving to toss in a new pair of pants for me and closed it. I pulled them on and caught a look at myself in the mirror. I looked older than I should have for being in my late 20's. My normally short black hair had gotten a bit shaggy. I usually wore it neat and clean, but with all the stress of the last few months, I had forgotten to get it trimmed. My green eyes, which could be a hit with the ladies from time to time, were circled with bags and a bit sunken. My normally pale skin was more pale, maybe ashen from lack of sun, but that could have been from the blood loss.

Looking at myself I began to wonder, maybe for the first time, just what the fuck I was doing with myself. My head was a mess. I felt Jim tug on the power one last time for whatever he was doing on the roof, and then I descended into a state of morose confusion. My thoughts and feelings jumbled together for a while. I had always followed Jim. His charisma and larger than life attitude had always made me want to emulate him. Following him, we had ended up together in organized crime. Our business oversaw gambling and whores and theft and you name it. The questions came to my mind, what good had we done? What good had I done? I could see myself killing more people in the last couple of weeks than in my whole lifetime. Their faces in my mind, their bodies lying where they had fallen. At the same time, the dream of the ancient god walking across the ocean to battle evil and darkness came to mind. It occurred to me that I might be the evil and darkness in the world.

I stared at that mirror for some time. Then a thought came to me, one I had never had before. I wanted to be better than what I was. It was almost a yearning, a pleading, *please be better than who you are.* As I looked at myself in the mirror, I decided then and there that I would be. I didn't know how really. Believing I didn't have much time, or so I thought then. As far as I knew, everyone but Jim would be dead in a few days. But there was one thing I could do. I could get our crew and our bullshit out of Maria's life.

Hearing Jim come in, I exited the bathroom and walked through the bedroom and out into the kitchen. He was sweating a little. I could feel the power on him more clearly now. It was stronger.

"We can't stay here you guys," I said. "Pack your things up. When Sean gets back we have to go somewhere else."

"Why? We're good here." Jim said plopping down on the couch. I glanced at Maria whose face was blank and before I could answer he said, "She'll be fine. Lanza doesn't know where we are."

"It's not just her. There are gangs in these buildings. Any of them could have seen us and ratted us out. The price on your head is enough for that." I replied.

"We'll only be here three more days. The shipment comes in then. It will be fine."

Jim and I locked eyes for a few seconds. We had argued in the past and he usually won. Once in a while though, I wouldn't back down. We would either fight until I lost bad, or he would give in. I guess he saw in the moment that that's where we were headed. "God damn it, Jake, today is not the day."

I knew I had won the test of wills almost before it had started. "When Sean gets back, we're leaving. Jim, get your shit together. Everyone, get your shit together." The room was quiet for a few seconds. With me and Jim at odds, the guys weren't sure what to do. Then Stark got up and started putting his stuff back in his bags. He picked up Jim's duffle from the floor and handed it to him.

Jim sighed as he stood up and started packing his stuff. "Where we headed Jakey?" His voice had a tone in it, almost a sneer, but one of giving up as well.

"I'm not sure. Anyone have a spot?"

Marty piped up, he had a wry grin on his face, "I think I know a place."

It was very brief but I saw a flash of relief on Maria's face. If we were going to die in the next few days, at least I had done one thing to be a different man.

Chapter 20

Caravan

We hit the road shortly after Sean and Lou arrived. We had a two-car caravan going. Marty, Red, Sean, and Lou in Marty's car. Stark, me, and Jim in Stitch's. Of course, my Buick had been left a total wreck on the foggy streets in the city. We were following Marty after having stopped for gas. He said he knew a place in Monterey that we could probably use and left it at that. Stark was driving with Jim riding shotgun. I was sitting in the back. The Chevelle had worn black vinyl seats. They were bench style with cuts and scrapes all over them. There were dirty stains in the seams. I had a lot of room in the back and was comfortable.

We rode in silence for a bit, then Jim turned and asked, "What was that back there Jakey? You sweet on Maria or something?"

I looked him right in the eyes. "You're a piece of shit, Jim." The unexpected words were like a slap. I could see the surprise on his face. Stark caught his breath, quietly, but we could still hear it. The words had not come out of nowhere either. I had been thinking for some time. If someone needed to say something he didn't like, it was usually me to do it. Even so, I was crossing the line insulting the boss like that and in front of Stark no less. "You're a piece of shit. Stark here, he's shit too. And so am I."

"You better watch yourself Jake or we can pull over right here and have a go." The anger was welling up in his face. I could see the tension in his shoulders. He was getting ready to bust me up like he had done many times in the past. Stark just kept his eyes on the road.

"Fuck you. Just think. We're engaged in a drug war, a DRUG WAR!" I shouted. Calming a bit, "Look, I'm with you until the end of this. I got your back. I'll die with you and the rest of the boys if necessary. But we're not dragging some innocent woman and a child into this. Got it?"

For a second I could see him deciding what to do. Did he need to stop this rebellion? Did he need to show me, all of us, who was boss? Then Stark grunted in agreement and nodded his head. "Jake's right."

Jim looked to Stark, then back to me. I saw that slight smile cross his face again. "Ok bro, you got it. We'll keep Maria and everyone else out of this. Just watch your mouth. I don't want to have to shut it for you."

"Fair enough. Another thing though. If I survive this, I'm done. I'm out. We're not heroes here. We're not fighting some good fight. We're fighting to keep stealing and dealing and pimping on our terms. Just like we've always done since we were kids. I don't want it anymore." Having said what I had too, I went silent.

Jim gave me a long, blank look, then nodded and turned his head. Stark nodded as well, either in agreement or what, I don't know.

We drove the hours to Monterey. We made small talk along on the road almost as if the previous conversation hadn't happened. By the time we arrived the tension had left the car, mostly. We took some back streets driving through pines and bluffs until we ended up on a long driveway that took us to the top of a foothill. Directly at the head of the hill was a larger than average house, not a mansion but large, with sweeping views of the ocean a couple miles away. Jim started laughing.

"What's up boss?" Stark asked.

"Marty's brought us to one of Lanza's homes." He chuckled again. "As long as no one's here, they wouldn't even think to look for us in Monterey."

I said before, we had met Lanza at one of his homes around Marin County. He had more than one in San Francisco and a few throughout Marin. I even knew of a condo he owned in Los Angeles we had used when we went down there on business for him one time. It made sense he had another one in the sleepy tourist town a few hours from Frisco. I started to laugh too. It was risky but perfect if we didn't get caught.

Chapter 21

Respite

Now Marty was a typical Irish drunk, or so he seemed. He was taller than average with a tousle of hair that was red. It looked like an unkempt mop on his head. Wavy, almost curly, and with a reddish goatee it was his signature look. He had a bit of a beer belly, not huge on his tall frame but it testified to the fact that he always had a beer in hand. He could drink us all under the table, even Stark. Except for the belly, he was pretty lanky with long arms and thin fingers. What do his fingers have to do with it? Well, besides his appearance as a drunk, he was actually one of the better lock picks in San Francisco. He had become well versed in breaking in, shutting down security systems, opening safes, and that sort of thing. With those fingers, he could have been a guitar player. For us, he was in charge of our crew's B&E projects. It would usually be Marty and another of our guys and then a couple of younger ones like Sean or Lou on a job. He put those skills to use getting us into Lanza's house.

The first thing Marty did was walk around the home. We were told to wait by the cars while he inspected the doors, windows, and security features. He maybe spent twenty minutes doing that before pulling his tool bag out of the trunk and getting to work. A few minutes at one of the sliding glass doors in the back and he was in. Ten minutes later he opened the front door. The place was unlocked, and the alarm system deactivated. You might wonder why there wasn't better security. All I can think of is that this particular house wasn't used much.

Welcome to our new home." He said with a flourish of his hand and waved us in.

The Monterey house was opulent. It was furnished with some of the latest furniture, leather chairs and couches, glass and brass end tables and other luxury items. It was nice. The backside of the house, which faced the ocean, was floor to ceiling windows and sliding doors. The views were breathtaking. You could see the distance to the ocean with gorgeous, green trees and small town in between. Crime does pay sometimes, at least for guys on top. Red walked into Lanza's master and claimed the bedroom for his own. We all laughed at his offhanded comment about how a greasy mick was going to rub a couple out in that bed and leave it for Lanza. Every one of us found our places to sleep in that house. Sean and Lou shared a room with bunk beds probably set up for kids or grandkids. The other guys took guest rooms. Everyone but me got a bed. I took the couch. It may have been more comfortable than the beds. We loved that place.

The first night we went to town and loaded up on groceries. We had tons of beer and whiskey. Marty, with a beer in hand, found Lanza's wall safe and spent a couple hours opening it up. Red and Stark cooked dinner while the rest of us began making plans for what was to come at The Wharf. Red had learned how to cook pretty good, well-done meals work with getting a lady to take her pants off, and Stark wasn't too bad either.

That first night set the tone for our visit there. We threw empty beer cans in the fireplace or pool out back. We broke empty bourbon bottles on the front patio and other things. Basically, we acted like idiot teenagers. After opening the safe, Marty brought us a gun and stacks of money. There were even car keys in that safe that went to a mint 1969 Corvette Stingray in the garage. It was a work of art with metallic blue paint, gleaming chrome, and black highlights on the hood. Red tossed me the keys and said it was a replacement for my Buick. We were like children, but I don't regret it. We knew our time there might be our last and if messing up that house was a final flipping the bird to The Boss, so be it. We had fun. And you know what? After Lanza's betrayal, we deserved it.

The next night was like the first. We were a bit hungover during the day, but that didn't stop Red and Marty from heading into town and scoring a couple of ladies. They were gone for a few hours, so we were starting to get worried. Then they showed up with their shirts un-tucked and lipstick on Marty's neck. They had been in town at one of those fancy seafood restaurants with a bar in it. You know the kind, brass and wood, lights kept low for ambiance, oil lamps at the table. After having lunch, they decided to get a few drinks in the bar. Red, the peacock that he was, struck up a conversation with a couple of women who ended up taking a liking to our two guys. They spent the missing hours in the ladies' hotel rooms. We all had a roaring laugh when they came in, grins and everything. I guess everyone knew the danger we were in and instead of having a last meal, we wanted a last party, one last time with our friends and crew.

That night, the drinking was in full swing and we had a poker game going. We had divvied up the bloody money and were using it. It was fun, the winner would be richer, but also have the problem of having to "launder" that money in a way we normally didn't. I got up to go to the bathroom, and while I was in there, I felt the tug or push or whatever it was when Jim used the power. As I was coming out, I could see the table had quieted down. Everyone was looking through the windows at Jim, who had gone out back. It was starting to rain, and he was just standing there head high, eyes cast out over the darkening coast, unhindered by the storm that was coming down around him. And, of course, he was mostly dry. He kept clenching his fists and every time he did, I felt the power. A few seconds later something would happen, the rain would get heavier or lighter, the wind would pick up, lightning might crash over the ocean. Because I could feel that power, I knew Jim was causing those changes. He was practicing.

As I came out and headed back to the table the guys looked away from him. They had been talking but stopped when I entered. A couple of them looked at their cards. A few glanced at me guiltily. They knew something was up. At that moment, I wondered if they could feel the power too. Most wouldn't keep eye contact with me. Red did, though, and I could see a determined look on his face.

"What's up with Jim?" He asked.

I sat down and took a shot of bourbon one of the boys had refilled for me. "Whatta you mean, bro?" I said, trying my best not to look surprised. I might have over slurred my words. I had been drinking, but not that much. I picked up my cards.

"Don't give me that crap, Jake. We know something's up with Jim. One of the whores from Butchertown said she saw Goldfinger stab him. She said some other stuff too, not that I believe it, but ya know, we know he's different."

"We heard about the door at the restaurant too. Some password." Stark looked up from his cards. His face was almost impassive, almost, but I could see the knowing in his eyes. He discarded some cards and was dealt replacements. Sean, who had been with us at the bottom of the restaurant, stared at his cards intently.

Lou was looking between me and the crew. He was a bit puzzled and didn't want to get in between us, more senior guys. Both Sean and Lou folded, dropped their cards face down when Stark put five bloody bills into the pot.

"Look at him Jake, he's standing in the rain and he's dry. We're not stupid, man." Red pressed. Jim was still out there; his use of the power had taken on a different rhythm. It was slower with more prolonged pulls at it. He had stopped clenching his fists, but I could still feel it happening.

"How did he take on Crispy and all those guys by himself? Why wouldn't he take us with him?" Stark asked.

I held up my hand, "Alright, he's got an edge." It was clear they had thought about the last couple of weeks themselves. "That's all I can say about it. Jim's not stupid, though, do you think he would have taken on Lanza without something up his sleeve? An ace maybe?" I said this as I laid down my hand, three aces.

Stark shrugged. Marty spit. Red glared. The three of them threw their cards face down on the table in defeat.

"I can't say any more. It's not my place. If you want answers, take it up with him." I said as I pulled my winnings from the center of the table.

They never did ask, though. We kept playing and Jim came in a few minutes later to sit back down with us. I lost everything I had won that night. I think Stark ended up with all of the money.

Then we tied another one on.

The third night was more tense than the first two. We knew that the next day would be a battle for our ill-gotten shipment of drugs. We spent a few hours discussing our plans. They weren't super spectacular. First, Jim, I, Sean and Lou would head to Molloy's to pick up some weapons. We had a stash there. Marty, Red, and Stark would go to the bank to get our money and stolen jewelry out of the safety deposit boxes. We wanted some resources with us in case things went bad and whoever was left made a run for it. We would all meet near The Wharf. Stark, who in his younger years had done a stint in the marines, would take a rifle to a rooftop near Pacific Crab and the dock we expected the boat to come in on. Marty and Red would take up positions halfway between Stark's rooftop and the seafood business. Keeping an eye out and being able to help either of us if we need it. While they all did that, Jim and I would sneak into the building and force the employees there to use the radio to divert the boat to a different dock. We would try and take our shipment without bloodshed.

We knew that was a long shot, of course. We knew this was likely to be a fight bad enough that most if not all of us would die. I knew Jim probably wouldn't, but still, like I said it was tense. Jim even offered to let whoever wanted out, to take their share of our money and things and leave the city. No one did. We were all in it until the end.

So, we made a good last meal, played some more poker, insulted each other, drank a bit, and generally enjoyed the camaraderie that men often do in trusted circles. It was a good last night.

Chapter 22

Final Dream

I dreamed a final vision again that evening, the final dream for this story anyway.

This time the setting was the same, the stars in the sky, the sun and moon, the ocean and crescent beach. There, the darkness cascading across the landscape, swallowing it up. The darkness flicking out tendrils of black void to assail us. The dream was different, though. This time I was not on the beach. This time I was the ancient man, ancient god, walking across the water. This time I wore fire and light like a crown. This time the light from my eyes illuminated all and saw everything. The powers of creation were mine to command. I cannot describe it except to say that those energies, as real to me in that dream as you are here at this table, fed me and grew from me.

To my left and right, my companions walked with me. All six, old beings of aeons past, fueled and fueling the same fires that burned around us and in us. All were aware of me, but only one looked, glancing quickly. It was the beautiful woman to my right, tan-skinned, almost olive, wearing nothing but a gold skirt. She smiled, and her smile was short, but in that moment, I felt like I was being welcomed. It showed nothing of the horror we were about to face. Her gold skirt was actually very thin, beaten gold plates strung together in rows down to her ankles. I could see a gold ankh hung between her breasts, which, were perfect, as was the rest of her form. I mention her form only to speak of this: All seven of us were physically perfect.

Glancing at the figures walking with me I could see nothing but magnificence. Even through the clothes, muscles rippled and forms moved with purpose and grace. To say I had never seen such fluid motion would be an understatement. I knew instinctively that we represented the perfection of creation.

When I dreamed, I didn't know what an ankh was. I do now. Anyway, that doesn't matter I guess. What happened next was that seven columns of darkness stretched towards us and we were all engaged in battle. Each lance of the void contained a being as imperfect as we were perfect. They were as fueled by destruction as we were by creation. I guess you could say they were destruction perfected if there is such a thing. Only one was man-shaped and he had a tentacle coming out of one eye. The rest were things too difficult to describe, bubbling globs of ooze that shifted and reshaped as we fought, animals and beasts of unknown origin. We fought and grappled with those things.

As we punched and stabbed at them, as we launched fire and thunder and spears of ice into the darkness, they whipped tentacles and tore with fangs, they hurled columns of smoke and void and other things I can only describe as empty. Things that had form and hurt us but were made of energies or substance that swallowed our beings. It was strange, sometimes our powers would harm them, other times they would be swallowed and make our enemies stronger. And as we fought, I became aware of the void that fueled them. I could see into it, see that it wasn't just an empty abyss. Within it existed stars, but they were opposite of ours. They swallowed light and gave the beings we fought a power of emptiness. There were worlds and landscapes like the ones we fought to protect, but they supported imperfection maybe. I don't know. It remains a paradox to me, something I cannot understand even though I have tried.

I awoke alone on that couch. Everyone was asleep except Jim. He sat out in the back unaffected by the cold morning weather. His back was to me. But when I woke up, I was left with an understanding of some things. The first was that the war was real. It was ancient, as old as time. I also understood that it could not be won. Battles in that war might go to a victor, but the war was never-ending. Finally, it came to me that while the war could not be won, it must be waged. It's an interesting thought, an enlightenment almost, that some fights don't exist to have a winner. They exist simply to be fought.

Chapter 23

Gearing Up

After I woke up, I started the coffee and took a shower. I guess my noise woke some of the other guys up too. Or maybe everyone had slept poorly considering the tension the day held. Stark and Red were in the kitchen making breakfast when I came out. Jim was still sitting outside, but I could see a cup of joe steaming on the table next to him. I could hear at least one or two of the other guys moving about in the back. About ten minutes later Stark started bellowing that breakfast was ready. The two of them, Stark and Red, put a nice breakfast spread out like something you would see on a guy's camping trip. There were plenty of scrambled eggs, bacon, sausage, and lots of toast. Jim walked in and the rest of the guys came from their spots in the house. We all sat down and had a good meal.

At one-point, Marty started to open a beer. Stark looked up and told him no drinking until after today.

"Fuck you, Old Man. You do today your way, I'll do it mine." He replied. The rest of us laughed while Stark looked on, then he grinned and laughed too. For a moment at least, it dispelled the worry we all felt. I'll say this for Marty, though, he only had the one beer.

After that, we packed our things and left. Marty, Red, and Stark went in one car. Sean and Lou took Stitch's. I pulled the Stingray around and Jim

111

hopped in the passenger seat. It was a cold day with a few clouds. We put the top down anyway. Leaving a bit after the other guys, our instructions to Sean and Lou were to be careful but meet us at Molloy's.

We took our time on the way back. The boat wasn't supposed to dock until later in the evening. The plan was to get to The Wharf at twilight and do what we had to do, a few hours before it was supposed to be there.

Partway into the drive, Jim said without looking at me, "Make sure you stick close to me Jakey. I'll do what I can to keep you alive."

"What about the other guys? They're our friends."

He just shrugged. "I'll do what I can for them too, but I want you nearby. Make sure you're always close to me."

"Yeah, sure." With a barbed tone. I didn't like the idea of our friends dying.

"I mean it. Until this is over, we're attached at the hip. All this will be meaningless for me if something happens to you. Got it?"

"I got it." I meant it too. I liked the idea of me dying even less.

He just nodded. "Good. I know you've got some problems with me right now. I'm OK with that. We'll work it out after our situation is solved."

"You know if whatever you have doesn't hold, both of us, all of us, are probably going to be dead."

"Don't worry, the power will be there. I'm not sure how to describe it, but we worked it out." Was his answer.

"Worked it out?" I asked.

He just shrugged.

We drove in silence most of the way back after that. Each in our own thoughts. I could feel him tug on the power lightly from time to time, for what reason I don't know, but that was it.

We entered San Francisco and made our way to Molloy's. The plan was to park in the alley and enter from the back door. As we got closer, I slowed down and both of us started scanning the street for any of Crispy's thugs. Suddenly, while we were doing that, we heard gunshots up ahead near the bar. I gunned the engine towards the alley about half a block up and cranked the wheel taking our stolen ride right into it. Up ahead we could see Stitch's car parked. In front of it, there was a trash dumpster and Sean and Lou were behind it. Sean was lying in a pool of blood while Lou kept popping up and firing shots down towards the other street. At the far end of the alley, thirty or forty feet from the dumpster was another car and on the other side of it, four of Crispy's guys were shooting at Sean. He was laying partially behind the dumpster with his head exposed to them. You could see him trying to lift his gun to shoot back.

I raced the car down that alley until we were closer and then slammed on the brakes. As I reached for my gun, blue light filled the cab. Jim's eyes were blazing bright. He had pulled himself up to a crouch in the seat. As the Corvette came to a stop he jumped. It was incredible. The car bucked from the force, but he leaped clear from our stopping car all the way to the end of that alley.

I can still see it in my head now. It was like something out of a comic book. He sailed above that dirty, trash-strewn alley, eyes shedding blue light all over the place. For a couple of seconds, the length of time in the air, the shooting stopped. Everyone's eyes were wide with shock, mine, Lou's, the guys on the other side of the car. We were all stunned as we watched him travel in a high arc, past the brick walls of the buildings, and slam down onto the street or sidewalk behind the other shooters. What kind of force does it require to launch a man over that distance? For that matter, what kind of strength does it take to kick in a metal, barred security door? I don't know. I do know the human face is not built to withstand it. Jim swung a mighty fist at one of the guys. I could hear the impact from where I was starting to get out of the car. It was the crunching sound of bones breaking and flesh tearing as his knuckles connected with the dude. There was a spray of blood as fragments of jaw and cheekbone got pushed into the guy's brain and erupted all over the vehicle. I don't think he had time to scream. He just flopped back against the car, faceless, breaking a window. Then he fell to the ground out of view.

Lou just stood there eyes wide, mouth open in astonishment, watching. He saw everything. Jim low kicked another one and we could hear the leg bones snap. As the man fell, his head was also broken open by another fist on the way down. Another spray of blood washed the car. The last two started screaming and firing in panic. I don't know how many times they hit him, two, three, maybe four, but there were bursts of blue fire and light every time the bullets found their mark. It didn't stop the onslaught. He moved to the other two, killing one as he had the first men. The last one died when Jim lifted him up over his head and slammed the man on his back on the car hood. Jim followed with a downward punch to the chest shattering sternum and rib cage. Blood came out of the man's mouth. We could hear some screams of fear from whoever was on the street at the time.

Jim was covered in the bone chunks and insides of our enemies. It was a frightening sight, a man standing there, dripping crimson blood and fragments of jaw while supernatural light poured from his eyes. He bent down behind the car, and as he stood back up the light faded, and his normal gaze returned. He had torn a jacket off one of his victims. Walking towards us, he tried wiping the blood from his hands with the ripped fabric, not that it did much good. There was death all over him. I could see the car behind, dented from impacts and dripping with ichor from the carnage.

Lou started to stutter. He looked at Jim with absolute terror. By that point, Jim had dropped his makeshift rag, removed his own jacket, and was wiping dead men's blood from his face. Then he walked into Molloy's.

Lou was looking at me, eyes wide with fear. "I, I, I don't know if I can do this."

I was checking Sean, who was still alive and had used my own jacket to press against the wound. Sean was nearly unconscious. I don't know if he witnessed any of what just happened.

"Listen," I said loudly, as Lou was still stuttering. "Sean needs a hospital. You need to get him there."

"I can't do this." Lou's eyes were glassy and far away, his words were vacant, hollow.

"You can get Sean to the hospital." I grabbed his wrist and pulled him down to Sean. Together we lifted him up. I threw one of Sean's arms over Lou's shoulders and said, "You need to go. Go quickly. Head to Donagan's or the ER. Whatever you do, get him some medical attention."

Lou started walking towards the Chevelle, hefting his friend, helping him walk as best he could. Sean's feet were nearly dragging. His eyes were blurry, and he was wheezing.

Watching Lou go, seeing the look of terror on his face, it dawned on me there was something else I could do. He was a few years younger than me, not much, but looking at him it felt like there was a gulf of age between us. We older folks had led him into this path, a younger man, vulnerable to the bad in the world like we had been, bad we had eventually become. Maybe before I died there was one more good act I could perform. Perhaps a further testament to my desire to be different. Reaching into one of Jim's duffles and pulling out a roll of $100's, I called for Lou to stop.

"Here," I said as I pushed the money into his free hand. He couldn't speak but his eyes were pleading with me. "This is for you and Sean, if he makes it. And Lou, it's OK. Get him to a hospital, and if we never see you guys again, it's OK."

Relief washed over his face. Even so, I figured he would have nightmares about that day for weeks. Hell, I did.

After finding Jim in Molloy's, we stocked up. When we came out with our bag of weapons, Lou and Sean were gone. They had left Stitch's Chevelle for some reason, probably shock. I never found out why, though.

Chapter 24

The Shipment

We had a few hours before our meeting with the shipment. Having thrown our weapons and spare cash in the trunk, I drove the Corvette around until we found a shitty run-down hotel. You know the kind, one of those little shit holes in big cities. They usually have names like The Regency or King's Palace or something. This one was called The Royal. It was dirty and old and like most buildings in San Francisco, it was built touching its neighbors on either side. I went in and got us a room while Jim hunkered down in the car out of sight. He was still bloody. His hair was matted and stuck to his head and that was after cleaning himself up and picking bone fragments from his hair. I let him in the back so no one would see us. We went to our room and there he showered and changed clothes.

After that, I insisted we go shopping for new suits. He thought it was stupid, and maybe it was. Maybe it was my vanity, but I thought if I was going to die that day, I wanted to meet my maker looking as good as possible. First impressions and all that, right? Anyway, we ended up at a fairly high-end store and got some nice clothes. They weren't as good as the tailored things we were used to wearing, but we didn't have time for those. When we were packing up, as an afterthought, I picked out a couple of wool trench coats, slightly over-sized. They were black and went well with the charcoal herringbone threads we had just

118

put on. With white shirts, blue ties, our suits, and the coats, we looked good.

By then it was time. We went to our meeting place with Red, Marty, and Stark. It was a few blocks up from The Wharf. We pulled into an alley and the five of us gathered around the trunk of the Stingray. There we got out our weapons. Stark took an old rifle we had, the type he had used when he was young. It was a US military surplus from Korea or Vietnam. I don't know. Marty took a shotgun. Red took some extra pistols. Jim and I, well we took Tommy guns, you know, Thompson sub-machine guns. Don't make that face. I told you earlier what happened at The Wharf was gangland. Just because those things were the favorite of the mob in the 20's doesn't mean they weren't still in use. Ours had been stolen off a US navy boat around the same time Stark had been in the service. They were prone to jams and that sort of thing, but generally, they got the job done.

From there, Stark was dropped off at a building about half a block from our target, Pacific Crab. It was along the road that ran parallel to the ocean and one could see all the piers jutting out from the top of it. His rifle concealed in a duffle; he made his way up the fire escape on the outside of the structure. It was still daylight, but twilight had just started to descend.

We checked around The Wharf, looking for any of Crispy's guys, but didn't see any. Following a bus closely, when we got near the business I gunned the engine and pulled up to the right of the big vehicle. It shielded us from view of the rest of the street. As we neared the crab building, I pulled farther to the right

Aaron Ross

and parked on the ocean side. I was hoping that no one from the street would see the car parked unless they were close. Jim and I were out of the car in a flash. Our Tommy guns hidden underneath our trenches, we quickly pushed our way into the building, entering through the warehouse portion. A couple of workers were boxing up crab. We walked right by them and opened the door into the office area. Our target was there.

His name was Mike something or other, the nameplate on the desk. It was one of those old green sheet metal things, starting to rust from the ocean air. Each side was a set of drawers that look like filing cabinets. Then it had the metal top with a fake wood veneer. Papers were all over the top. They had crab numbers and shipping manifests and the like. On the right side of the desk was a big block radio, gray and also rusted, with one of those handpieces that had a button to click. Jim pulling the heater from his trench, put the muzzle of the Tommy to the man's head and lifted a finger to his slips to signal silence. Then he nodded for me to check the rest of the office.

I went through the building. Only one other person was there, and he was in the break room drinking a coffee and reading a paper. Apparently, the noise of the bus or other traffic had masked the sound of our car and entry. I recognized him immediately as one of Mustache's old crew. His eyes went wide as he saw me and reached for his gun. I was across the room before he could draw it out and rammed the barrel of my machine gun right into his mouth. As his head reeled back, I swing the butt of the weapon and smashed him across the side of his head. He went down, unconscious and missing a few teeth. I looked out the window from that room. I could see Marty and Red down the street. Stark was visible on a rooftop maybe 100 yards from our position. Our plan seemed good. Everyone was in position.

"We're clear". I called to Jim as I pulled the partially unholstered pistol from the thug's hands and slid it into the small of my back.

"Now," I heard Jim start, "There's a boat coming in tonight. It's scheduled to get here at 11:15. It's called the Frisco Whaler and it's one of the boats you get crab from."

"Yeah?" I could hear Mike's voice crack a bit from fear and recognition.

"I want you to divert it to pier 30," Jim answered. We were at Pier 23. What you may not know is that the SF piers all line what's called the Embarcadero. Many, like Pier 39 have become tourist destinations with restaurants and shops and lots of other things. Others, like Pier 30 are parking lots. Some are good for fishing or walking along. Some are used for business. Also, the odd numbers stretch off to one side from the main Ferry Building. It's central to the piers. The even-numbered piers run along the other side. This put Pier 30 a pretty good distance from 23.

Something on Mike's face or maybe his tone caused Jim to ask the question, "What is it? What's the matter?"

"Crispy was here earlier. He sent a speedboat out to the Whaler. It's empty." It was clear Mike knew what was going on. He had been at the business a while and was considered a low-level employee of The Family.

"Damn it." I heard Jim say quietly. Then there was a crack as he buttstroked Mike with the Tommy gun. Footsteps followed as Jim entered the room I was in.

"Is Mike dead?" I asked.

"I don't think so. I went easy." Was Jim's reply. "Looks like Lanza or Crispy out thought us. They beat us to our shipment. We're going to have to get it somehow."

So, what had happened was that Crispy sent a boat out to meet the Frisco Whaler. They had taken our shipment in, many hours before it was due, hours before we had tried to do something similar.

"Let's get out of here," Jim said. "We'll figure out another..."

As he was talking, we heard gunshots. I looked out the window and saw a flash or two on the rooftop. Stark had stood up and was taking aim at somebody that I couldn't see. In the darkening twilight, every time he pulled the trigger there was a flash. You could see other lights, from other guns and their quieter reports even though you couldn't see the shooters.

Now I told you before. You don't fuck with a guy like Stark. Stark was an older dude. He had a little extra weight on him from too much food and drink.

But The Old Man was also strong. He had muscles on him from years back. He had been a marine in Korea or Vietnam, I don't know which. As a marine, the man served some tours in combat zones. Eventually, he became a boxer for the corps. His skills had been quite good too. The marines pulled him out of combat and made him one of their fighters, fighting the Army, Navy, and Air Force boxers. Unfortunately, and this is what led him to our crew, he was dishonorably discharged for knocking an officer out. He got caught getting busy with the officer's wife, a fight ensued, and of course Stark won. In the military, enlisted men don't often win legal battles against officers. The brass protects its own. So Stark was discharged with a felony. He couldn't vote and had other restrictions. His way to make money and feed himself was to join the San Francisco underworld. Years later he was still with us. His sandy hair had turned to gray. His well-muscled form covered in a bit of pork from drinking and old age. But he was still Stark.

I don't know how many guys followed him up that fire escape. We couldn't see how many he dropped. We didn't see much from our vantage point. Stark shot a few times. Then we saw him moving, and two guys were on him. That we could see. His rifle dropped and he was swinging those heavy hands. One of the two guys had a pistol and fired it wildly. It looked like two of the shots hit him in the gut. The effects could be seen on him, but suddenly he had a hatchet in his hand. Where it came from, I don't know. How he could still be standing, I don't know. But he swung it at one guy and took a hand off. The flashes of light kept going off. Then the three of them fell to the ground out of view. We saw another flash of light. We saw that hatchet raise one more time. Then we didn't see anymore.

"Fuck," Jim said, expressing what we both felt. I could see Red had started to move towards Stark's building but stopped at the last. He could see what we saw.

At that point, we heard some screeching tires on the street. The gunfire was heard up and down the road and people and cars had at first looked, then started clearing out. Most people run when they hear bullets, and they should. The sound of tires skidding to a stop was from four vehicles that had come out of the buildings opposite the ocean. Crispy and his guys were parked at various angles on the street. They were pouring out of the cars and setting up to use them for cover. It was an ambush and they must have seen Jim and me somehow. Parked a little ways down the road, it was possible the Stingray was visible from where they had entered the Embarcadero. Whatever happened, it was clear our presence and position had been blown.

Marty started firing as he ran to our building. Red did as well. The shotgun took a guy down in the first blast. Red was shooting with two pistols, gunslinger like, as he ran for the cover of our building. Marty was ahead of him and made it. Red, at least twenty yards behind, was not so lucky. Crispy and his guys had Tommy guns, AK47's, and other machine guns. Three of them opened up on Marty and Red. Red got hit and fell to the pavement.

Jim was in the process of breaking a window to fire back. Suddenly he shouted to get down and tackled me. As we went to the floor, he knocked the table in the room over, dragged me behind it, and lay on top of me. While he did this, the thundering noise of I don't know how many guns, too many, started. The machine guns outside jack-hammered a storm of bullets into our building. Glass broke, fragments of sheetrock fell on us, chairs and desks inside were torn to ribbons. The table was no help as bullets went through it after having already traveled out of the wall. Miraculously, neither of us was hit.

When the shooting died down Jim yelled at me to run. We sped through the building out the way we had come. The whole place was a wreck, the office portion at least. As we passed his office, Mike could be seen sagging in his seat where Jim had left him. The man had a couple of bullet holes in his body and blood was rapidly spreading across the floor. We passed through the warehouse and out to the Corvette. The workers from the crab machines were nowhere to be seen. Marty was outside, sandwiched between the building and our car. We hunkered down next to him.

Our first plan was to fire up the Stingray and take our chances on the road. That didn't work. Before we even got into the car, some of the shooters had swung wide so they could see the back of the building. As soon as they did, they started shooting. They tore the Corvette up. Glass shattered, holes covered the front, and vehicle fluids started pouring onto the ground. Jim and Marty both got hit. Marty in the arm as he swung his shotgun up. Jim in the chest. The bullet had no effect on him of course. There was just fire and light. He and I stood up as one and began firing. I'm sure it would have made a good scene in a movie. He was in the lead, I followed behind and to his right, using him as cover. Both of us had lifted our weapons and began to let loose in tandem. Those Tommy guns barked and spit fire, our trench coats flapping in the breeze behind us. A couple of our enemies went down. Then Marty was up on the other side of Jim, shooting a pistol with his good arm. He had dropped his shotgun. Some more men swung wide to take shots at us. Three, four, five, six, maybe more, we mowed them all down. Their bodies hitting the ground, hot, gun barrels sizzling in the pools of blood.

Guys kept pouring to the side, though. As we slowly walked up along the building firing, we kept taking them down. Then I saw something that fills me with dread to this day. Remember Vic? I told you about him. He was with Crispy and swung wide. He didn't have a gun. He had a bazooka or rocket launcher or something. Jim was in the process of reloading and just as Vic came round, my gun emptied as well. Vic fired. He missed us, but the Stingray exploded. The three of us were thrown forward by that blast as the rocket found its mark. Jim landed on his feet. I was smashed into the building. My ears were ringing, and I couldn't see for a few seconds. Jim was unfazed. He finished reloading his gun and started firing again. Through my blurry vision, I saw Vic dodge out of sight and escape his bullets, but others went down. Then the firing stopped.

Kneeling beside me, Jim said, "You OK?" He shook me gently and I came back to my senses. I could barely hear, but my vision cleared. I was in pain with cuts all over me. Pieces of metal and glass were lightly embedded in my arm, leg, and back. I looked over and saw Marty's lifeless form. He had been closer to the car, but not by much. He was unluckier than I. A torn piece of license plate had embedded itself in his head going halfway through it, including an eye socket. His remaining, vacant eye stared at me. What was left of the Corvette was smoldering and a piece of it was on its side.

Jim stood up. He could see through the holes in the building to the other side of the street. As soon as he did and looked, the gunfire started again, this time trying to take his head off. He dropped back down. He looked at Marty and then to me. "Cover me." He said.

With that, he closed his eyes and clenched his fists. I could feel him pull the power. It was stronger than ever. The winds picked up. Above us in the almost completely dark sky, clouds rolled in. Then impossibly fast a thick bank of fog rolled out of the ocean and covered The Wharf, maybe the whole city. It was thicker than any fog I had seen. Visibility was maybe five feet. It was incredible. I heard cries of alarm from Crispy and his guys. Then the firing started again, but it was wild. They couldn't see or hear us.

"I need to get you out of here." Jim, eyes blazing, said hoisting me up and handing me my Tommy. "Load up, we're going to run for it."

"They'll see you, Jim." I pointed at his eyes. The blue light was scattering all over the fog.

"It can't be helped. You need the mist." He said. I learned then that some things are not natural and the power requires continuous use to hold them in place. "Swing wide from me, go ahead, I'll finish them off."

I did as I was told and ran a quick jog to the side of the building. Jim followed, but as he turned the corner of the building the gunfire started. With that blue light flaring out, you could see him, even forty or fifty feet away. I saw bursts of fire and light as he was hit. His gun answered theirs and you could see the muzzle flashes of all the weapons mutely through the mist. Then I decided not to run. I had said I was in it until the end and meant it. I moved up quickly to the side, where I could see Crispy and his guys' guns going off, flanking them.

Then it happened. Vic let go with his rocket launcher again. He hit Jim squarely. I could see and feel the explosion, though I was too far from it to get knocked down. There was a ball of explosive fire, followed by blue and I could just for a moment see Jim's silhouette being torn apart in the mist. The blue light blazed on. His body, where it lay, was still infused with power and pulsed with the supernatural. He wasn't moving, and the mist began to recede.

In fury, I screamed and charged towards the remaining men. They were surprised as I came out of the mist. I'm not sure how many were there, I just kept firing into the dark. They fired back and I found myself out of ammo behind one of their cars. The Tommy gun was empty. Drawing both my pistol and the one taken earlier, I decided to go out gunfighter style like Red.

"Jake is that you?" I heard Crispy call, then he laughed. "Jim is fucked man, I don't know what he is, but grenades do the trick. Once we're done with you, we'll finish him off." Then I heard him say to Vic, "Reload and hit that car." He meant the one I was behind.

From my vantage point, I could see the blue glow of Jim's body start to ebb. I could feel the power there, but it was receding, dying off.

"Not tonight Crispy, you stupid, fucking, runt." I heard Stark say. I heard running footsteps and stood up. Suddenly, out of the fading mist came The Old Man. He was firing a pistol in one hand and swinging his hatchet in the other. There were at least six or seven guys left. Stark charged them all. He was bleeding profusely from his gut. There was red wet all down the front of his pants. But somehow, he was there. Maybe the most loyal man I have ever met, he had crawled down that fire escape with bullets in his gut and heavy blood loss to help us. I joined the rush forward, firing as well. One thing was for sure, if we were going to die that night, Crispy was too.

Stark beat me to him. He came in, shot one guy, brushed past his falling body and sank his hatchet deep into Crispy's torso. Blood spurted everywhere. The Old Man was a tough son of a bitch. The problem is, for anyone, everyone really, no matter how tough you are, if you get hit with a shotgun you're pretty much done. I had killed a couple of Crispy's guys myself, but three were still up. One shot Stark in the head with a 12 gauge at point black range. I watched him fall. Loyal, tough, by all accounts a good man to have at your back. Maybe even more than Jim, Stark was my hero.

I continued firing and screaming with impotent rage. Vic swung around with his cannon and let loose. Had he hit me, we both would have been dead I was so close. As it was, he hit the car a ways behind us. The explosion was far enough back to knock us down, but not do too much damage. As angry as I was, I just kept firing as the four of us fell. I could barely see but I was determined not to stop. When my guns were empty, I realized that I had been the only one making noise. Laying there, half-unconscious on the asphalt, bloody, beaten and bruised, my vision cleared and showed that almost everyone around me was deathly still. The mist had mostly receded, and the faint blue light glowed on the other side of Crispy's cars.

I was alone.

Chapter 25
Finale

As I stood up and turned to face where Jim lay, my eyes swept over the carnage. Crispy was gasping and bleeding out with Stark's hatchet sticking out of his chest. Stark himself was long gone after most of his face had been erased by the shotgun. I could tell it was him, but whoever cleaned up this mess would have a hard time making an identification. Vic, the guy with the rocket launcher was dead. I had pounded at least four holes in his chest. Not even a whisper of air escaped his lips. To keep my promise, I shot Crispy in the head silencing him forever. It was a needless afterthought really, as I walked to Jim. He wouldn't have survived anyway.

Jim was somehow clinging to life, blue light pouring from his eyes and mouth. His blood, a glowing blue ichor, turned a crimson color as whatever power animated him ebbed the farther it flowed from his body. Jim was in worse shape than I could have imagined. His left arm and upper left torso were completely gone. His left leg remained barely attached to what was left of his shattered pelvis. Every hole in his body glowed with that blue light. The shrapnel cuts on his legs, face, and only arm glowed, even the partial lung I could see laboring for breath.

His right hand, still functional, held the stone glowing brighter still. He silently reached out to me. I rushed to his side, sickened in the knowledge that whatever power he held, it was not great enough to save him. His hand found mine, and there between our two palms, the stone felt warm, blazing with blue and gold light. A force flowed into my body from that stone, an ancient power long forgotten to man. I could hear whispers, indiscernible as if quietly spoken to the wind, but I heard them there just the same. As the power entered my body, it also entered my mind. It gave Jim a last wish, a final communication to me, and that's how I know what happened down in Colombia.

As Jim's power began to flow into me, my mind was transported to the jungle of a few months before. There I saw the ambush of Jim, and Mustache, and Vaccaro. How the rebels came out of the jungle all but invisible until their guns started firing. Jim was shot in the leg but made it to the tree line and fell into the deep green leaves. He only heard the screams behind him for a few minutes, and then he was too deep in the jungle, or maybe the rest were dead. It didn't matter. Jim ran and continued running. He moved on, perhaps for hours, limping on that wounded leg, only stopping briefly to cinch his belt above the bullet hole.

He was lost in that jungle for four days.

By the time dawn of that fourth day rolled around, Jim was delirious from lack of food and the infection that had set into his leg. He was only walking, slowly limping as best he could, but for all he knew he had been going in circles. After a few hours, he couldn't walk anymore and fell to his knees. He heard sounds on the wind that were like voices he couldn't make out. The same ones that showed me his story. He crawled in the direction of those voices and after some time came across a stone structure, a stepped pyramid. I guess educated people would call it a ziggurat. The voices came from the top and he knew, if he were to survive, he had to make it up there. So, Jim did. He crawled up those vine and dirt-covered steps. A true test of will, if there ever was one. He climbed through the pain of his leg, through the stink of the puss dripping infection, through the heat, the exhaustion, and hunger. Step by painful step, he crawled to the top.

And there he found no people, just a statue of an ancient man with a wreath of light around its head and lightning in the hands. Both the wreath and lightning were fashioned from a metal, gold or bronze. Before the statue was an altar thousands of years old and on that altar sat the stone. It was then as I saw it later, wrapped in wire and on a leather thong. It pulsed blue then and Jim grabbed it. As soon as he did the power flowed into him. His eyes shown bright and the wound on his leg healed. The energy melded with his purpose and filled his mind like water fills a cup. He drew himself up, proud and strong as I had always known him.

The last memory I have of Jim is from that dream. He stood tall atop the pyramid looking out across the jungle, black hair shining and blue eyes blazing. And my mind came back to The Pier.

It was at that point that the power chose me to take Jim's place. I could feel it settle in, comfortable having examined me. And as the blue light flowed from Jim's eyes into mine he breathed his last and sagged. I inherited a great gift that day, something unimaginable. But I also lost the only man I ever loved. I lost the only family I had left.

You see, my name is Jake, Jake Jones. I'm Jim's brother, and now I don't squint into the rain.

About the Author

Aaron Ross is a jack-of-all-trades. With a B.S. in Management Information Systems and an M.B.A. His skills are wide-ranging, from his multi-state real estate company, to his partnership in a boardgame/mobile app corporation, to his hand-dug pumpkin patch, Aaron's skills are in demand. Deciding to try his hand at something new, The Stone is his first foray into the world of writing. Also, he plays Dungeon's and Dragon's every other Sunday. What a nerd!

Aaron lives with his wife, Michele, and son, Connor, in Texas. Don't forget their cat, Max, and dog, Michigan!